The
Investment

Other Books by Douglas Shawn Blakeny II

3 Second Rule (self-improvement)
Shock-Up (fiction, to be released)

The Investment

by Douglas Shawn Blakeny II

Dedication

I dedicate this book to my family and friends. Thank you for the continued support! Love you guys....

Chapter 1

RJ ROBINSON SURVEYED the state campus again. From the small plaza where he stood, sidewalks spread like spider legs from all sides to encompass all parts of the campus.

Most of the dorms stood on the north side of campus, nestled between mature oaks and maples. The trees kept the rooms cool in the August heat. The upperclassmen typically stayed in the dorms nearer campus, while the freshmen had to live in the furthest outreaches of the spacious campus. Most of the classes were held on the southern side of campus. While these classrooms had been outfitted with the latest technology, they felt like they'd been around for decades, since they still had individual desks and chalkboards. On the eastern side of the campus were restaurants and bars, which RJ currently had no time for.

He couldn't believe this was real. Sure, he'd been here several times for campus visits and orientation, but school was actually starting now. For a few seconds, he just stood and watched all the people milling around him. Nobody really cared if you stared at them as they walked along the sidewalks, since their gazes were fixed on their phones. Two girls walked by, wearing the summer attire of shorts and midriff-exposing tops. A few boys walked by, just wearing basketball shorts and tennis shoes, but most of the guys wore polos and walking shorts.

He nearly bumped into a mother who was crying as her daughter entered the nearest dorm. She held a tissue to her eyes and barely acknowledged his behavior. The man next to her, presumably the father, mumbled something to RJ and patted his wife's shoulder.

The campus had been funded by the federal government centuries earlier—when land was cheap, and education was desperately needed. The colonists had the option of an education in England, or at one of the few universities in the newly formed states. While this campus had an official name, RJ had never heard it referred to as anything but State.

The State campus took up hundreds of acres of land. Dorms, academic buildings, and (eventually) stadiums had been strategically located along the tree-lined streets, which had once been cobblestone roads. RJ liked the history of the place and the spaciousness of the campus, unless he had to run across it to get to his next class.

As he observed the hundreds of freshmen around him, he felt at home. None of them knew him now, but within a few weeks, everyone would hear about his expertise on the football field. That much he did know. Scouts were already talking to his parents about him leaving school after a year or two and heading to the NFL. All he had to do was continue to play at his normal level, and the world would be his.

RJ had left his parents in the parking lot. They wanted to come with him, help him get settled, and go out for dinner together. But RJ knew that first impressions were important, and he didn't want to blow it with his new teammates by looking like a mama's boy.

So the week before, he asked his father to rent a truck, and they moved all of the furniture into his dorm room. It had been smaller than he thought it would be, and they'd actually had to take some of the things he'd brought back home. Now he only had a few suitcases with him, and after summer training, carrying suitcases was as easy as carrying a few books.

He'd spent part of the summer on campus, running daily and going to practice twice a day. The routine had been good for him. He'd put on some more muscle and lost a little of the extra weight he'd put on during the off-season. Between the Connecticut winter and the spate of graduation parties he'd attended, RJ had been guilty of too much cake and too little exercise.

RJ entered the doors to the residence hall. The noise level hit him like a linebacker. It was one of the all-male dorms on campus, which was mainly used by student athletes. So it sat nestled among the upperclassmen dorms, rather than out with the freshman dorms. Even on the first day of school, it smelled vaguely like a locker room. He recognized several of the guys from the football team in the hallways. They were in various states of undress, which made the dorm feel even more like an oversized locker room.

It was still mid-August, and while the dorm was air-conditioned, the constant influx of people and gear had made the building hot and sticky. He could already feel the trickle of sweat down his back. He'd need a shower before going to the cafeteria for dinner.

He greeted most of the guys with a nod. From their builds, RJ could easily tell that they were athletes, but he was bad with names. He recognized some of the faces from practices. But he was a starter for the team, and most of them weren't. He already had a good reputation on the team, and most of the other freshmen were walk-ons or third-stringers.

RJ knew his good fortune to be starting as a freshman, but he also knew that he'd worked hard to get there. It hadn't been easy for him, especially with the pressures at home. However, he knew that with hard work, most things were possible. And he'd kept that mantra alive throughout his high school days.

He passed two shirtless guys in the hallway, each carrying a can of beer. RJ was a little surprised. He was no stickler for the rules, but this was more blatant rule-breaking than he was used to. Sure, he'd had a few drinks at high school parties. Shit, who hadn't? But it was another thing to see guys without IDs openly carrying around beers.

After he made his way to his room on the second floor, he set his bags down, fished out his keys, and opened the door.

His roommate, Kevin, was already inside. He was leaning back on one of the beds, which looked like it had just been made, and he was listening to an iPod. He nodded as RJ came into the room and threw his bags on the bed.

"Sup?" RJ asked, nodding his head at the brute of a guy. Even though he was only second-string, he was buffer than anyone RJ had ever seen before. His upper arms were thick, muscled, and larger than some of his high school teammates' legs. He had a tattooed ring of barbed wire around his left bicep.

His pecs were evenly rounded like a model in a magazine. He had a deep ridge that ran down the middle of his midsection, and four lines separating his eight-pack. Try as he might, RJ had never gotten more than six. He was a little jealous that this guy could relax and still look that good.

Kevin popped one of the earbuds out and pointed at the desk. A new pair of LeBron X shoes were sitting on the desktop next to the second-hand computer that his parents had just bought him. "Those are for you," he said simply, then went back to his music.

RJ stepped closer and looked at the shoes. They were fine-looking kicks, but he had no idea where they'd come from. He couldn't afford shoes like that, and he knew the school's strict rules about buying gifts for athletes. So it hadn't come from the school either. He knew that some of the alumni got off on buying things for players, so he shrugged it off and stuck them under the bed. He would ask about the protocol for returning them later. RJ knew how much everyone was counting on him, and he didn't want to screw up their hopes and dreams.

RJ quickly unpacked, hanging clothes where they belonged. He didn't really have much. His parents weren't well-to-do at all. They were at the low end of the middle class, or what was left of it these days. He'd mainly worn jeans and sports t-shirts to high school.

He dumped socks and underwear in a drawer, and sat down on the edge of the bed, unsure of what to do next. Classes didn't start for two more days, and practice wasn't until 4 pm that day. (That way, it would be a bit cooler than it had been during the early-afternoon practices from the week before.) He thought about reading a book, but he didn't want to appear geeky in front of Kevin or the other players.

Kevin sat up on the bed and looked over at RJ. "There's a mixer over at one of the sorority houses tonight. Dude, you gotta come."

RJ thought about his girlfriend back home. He wasn't sure how she'd feel about a houseful of girls and (presumably) drinking. She could be jealous when she didn't like something. He weighed the situation over in his mind, but he could see Kevin measuring the time he was taking. He wished he could hurry up and answer, but he felt like Kevin would be judging him, based on this decision. RJ often felt like others were judging his behavior and performance, which often kept him on the straight and narrow. "Okay," he said finally, "but just for a little bit. I'm beat from traveling and moving."

Kevin raised an eyebrow at him. "Dude, you had four suitcases. Nothing to be tired about. Wait till you see some of the girls at the house. You'll perk right up, if you know what I mean." He laughed in a way that left nothing to the imagination.

RJ blushed a bit. He wasn't a prude, but he planned to stay faithful to his girl. He and Mya had talked about this a lot over the past two months, and they'd opted to give a long-distance relationship a try. Now RJ was already going out, and it was only his first night there.

Kevin ignored the blush. He grabbed his things and went down the hall for a shower.

RJ picked up his new phone. Even though it wasn't the latest model, it had been a present from his parents for graduation. He called Mya. She was his everything, and this was the first time they'd been away from each other since junior high, when they'd first started dating. It felt weird for her to be two hours away. Home seemed a lot farther away than it really was.

She didn't pick up, and RJ immediately jumped to all the worst-case scenarios. *She's met someone else. She's been hurt or killed.* He shook his head as if that would dislodge the thoughts. He was just under a lot of stress, and thinking this way wouldn't get him anywhere. He had to focus on the game. Mya wasn't going anywhere; he knew that in his heart, even if his head wanted to mess with him. The call went to voicemail, and he left a message for her to call back when she could.

At 4 pm, the practice went off without a hitch. He was getting used to the receivers and the other players. Every team held an entirely new set of circumstances and opportunities. He was worried about being such a young starter in their first game.

After practice, he headed back to the dorm alone. He sat on the bed for a while, wondering what to do. Soon, classes would start, and the season would begin shortly after that. But for now, he was bored. He looked at the shoes again, and put them in the closet. He would deal with them later. He wasn't going to be one of those athletes who only played for the money. He wanted to be remembered for his place in the game—what he accomplished in college and in the pros. That was what mattered. The rest was all show and bling. He didn't want to be a part of that. He knew that when the time was right, he'd get a paycheck that would keep his family wealthy for the rest of their lives.

Kevin came back, dripping wet. RJ wasn't pleased with the way he soaked the rugs and floor. This roommate thing was going to take some work. He was used to having his own space. RJ had been an only child, so he was used to everything being about him. Now he had to share with this guy, who had very different habits than his own.

Kevin turned to look at him. "So are you going to this party or what?" Kevin slid into a polo shirt, then stepped into some jeans without bothering with underwear. He must be confident about meeting girls if he wasn't even getting completely dressed. The thought made him rethink the mixer all over again.

RJ shrugged, which Kevin took for acceptance. The other athlete sprayed a heavy dose of cologne on his shirt and smiled. "Good. I can always use a wingman. You about ready?"

The sun had barely set, but Kevin looked ready to go. "They have some food there, and lots to drink. You can skip the dining-hall food tonight. For once, you'll have good chow." RJ didn't mind the cafeteria food here; the high school cafeteria had been all carbs and sugar. After all of his complaints, his parents had started shopping for protein-heavy meals to boost his metabolism.

RJ meekly followed the other guy down the hall and out into the quad. They greeted a number of people in the hallway, most of whom RJ hadn't met. But they all seemed to know Kevin. He fist-bumped and high-fived his way through the quad. As Kevin's friend, RJ got a few nods that he didn't get when he was alone.

The quad had four dorms, one on each side. A rectangular greenspace was in the middle, where students played Frisbee, worked on their tans, and studied. One of the dorms had been designated for the men's athletic teams, and the dorm opposite had been designated for the women's teams. The other two dorms were filled with upperclassmen who were more likely to party, but also more likely to know when to stop and get down to business. They'd made it through their first years, so they knew exactly what State expected from its students. RJ wondered if the upperclassmen had been placed there as an example for the freshman athletes.

Kevin led the way out of the quad and down Main Street. RJ hadn't learned the names of the cross streets yet, but he knew that he would eventually. On a quiet, tree-lined street named Oak, RJ could see flocks of students heading to a house about 300 yards away. The stereo system alone could have guided people there. RJ could hear the thump of auto-tune music as they approached.

The two-story house was labeled Omega Beta Zeta. RJ swallowed hard. He'd already been warned about this house from some of the guys on the team, and he'd heard other students talk about it in the locker room. It was the sorority for girls who liked to be popular and date athletes. RJ had heard stories about the girls here, which were almost told like ghost stories that could barely be believed. He had nothing in common with these girls, and thought about turning around to go back to the dorm.

However, two thoughts made him move forward: looking weak in front of his new roomie, and being alone and bored all evening. The crowd of people pushed up the front walk and into the house. Kevin hadn't been lying about the spread; it was great. The front entrance became a hallway that led to the backyard, where a dozen grills had been set up. Steaks, hamburgers, and hotdogs charred on the grills, and the smell of the food made RJ hungry. He'd been eating a lot over the last few days, since the long workouts in the heat made him constantly hungry. The coach was all for it, and encouraged them to eat four or five meals a day.

He split off from Kevin, who already had his arms around two girls. RJ didn't even know how he could meet them that fast. His roommate didn't seem to notice that RJ had headed off to the food, which was fine with RJ. While he was glad to have someone help him navigate through his first few weeks, he wasn't sure that he'd be friends with Kevin under any other circumstances. They were too different.

RJ piled his plate high with a steak, two burgers, and some potato salad. He found a picnic table toward the outside of the backyard area, where he sat down to eat and watch the crowd. He recognized a few of his teammates, but for the most part, the people here were strangers. He put his head down and focused on polishing off the food.

He looked up when a young woman sat down next to him. She slid close to him and put her hand on his arm. She definitely fit the sorority mold. She had lightly tanned skin, blonde hair, a big smile, and a tight T-shirt that barely contained her breasts. She was wearing cut-off jean shorts that left little to the imagination. "My name's Selina. You're RJ, right? I saw you practicing the other day."

RJ felt himself blush again, and he was glad that the twilight was masking the flush of his skin. He didn't want to seem like he was out of his element. He was going to be a big man on campus, the freshman starter for the football team. He had to start acting the part if he wanted to pull that off. He couldn't be tongue-tied every time he met a pretty girl.

"Yeah, that's me. Nice to meet you," he said, twisting his arm and holding his hand out to her.

She laughed slightly and shook his hand. Her grasp was firm, like she wouldn't easily let go. RJ let his hand go limp, and she got the hint, "Not what I was expecting in a starter."

She was leaning close enough toward him that RJ could feel her breasts against his arm, and smell the alcohol on her breath. *Not a good combination,* he thought. *I don't want to be hanging with a drunk tonight.* He made small talk with her as he finished his plate of food. Once he was done, he said his goodbyes and dumped the empty plate in the trash. She started talking to another athlete, and he breathed a sigh of relief.

RJ made his way out of the backyard and started through the house again. He had trouble finding his way to the front door, even though it had seemed fairly straightforward on the way in. The hallway was jammed with bodies, many of them pressed against each other. RJ was shocked at how blatantly some of them were yearning for a night of passion. He saw one guy with two girls, girls switching between guys, and even one guy with another. At that moment, he felt very sheltered. *Did all of this go on at home? Did Mya save me from the seamier side of fame?* He certainly hoped so, because none of it appealed to him at all.

He'd seen no signs of Kevin since the meal. RJ couldn't imagine that Kevin had skipped a meal and gone somewhere with those girls. They had a practice in the morning, and Coach would expect them all to be fresh and ready for practice. RJ respected the coach's opinion on the matter, and tried to live up to his expectations, just like he'd done for his grandfather.

RJ made his way through the crowd, avoiding the athletes who'd had too much to drink. Some of them were throwing up. A few were still standing and encouraging RJ to stay and "have some fun." He shook his head as he made his way home. RJ knew he was here for one reason and one reason only—to get picked by the pros and make some serious money in the NFL. Anything else was just a distraction.

He made it back to the dorm by about 10 pm. The hallways were clear and echoed with the emptiness of the building. RJ imagined that he could hear each step bounce off the walls.

He was tired and wanted a good night's sleep. He still hadn't adjusted much to the noise of the dorm. He was used to his own home, where things were quiet after 9 pm, and lights were always out by 11. From the weeks here this summer, he knew that he'd hear parties day and night. But he didn't know how those guys were going to study and stay on the team. There was too much at stake. If he went to bed now, maybe he'd be fresh for practice tomorrow.

RJ opened the door to his room and stopped just inside the frame. Kevin was buck naked on the bed. And he wasn't alone. He had two women with him, both just as naked as he was. They were the two girls from the party. One was kissing Kevin, while the other was running her hands over his body. RJ stood there frozen. He wasn't sure what to do.

Kevin turned and looked at him over his shoulder. "Dude, the sock is on the doorknob. Don't you know to stay out? Not sharing tonight. Maybe some other time, okay?"

RJ looked down. There was a white athletic sock dangling from the door. Apparently, it meant that he was supposed to stay outside. Damn, he still had a lot to learn.

Kevin was with two women! What the hell is up with that? RJ had only been with Mya, ever.

Out in the hallway, he slumped to the floor, stretched his legs out in front of him, and decided to wait until Kevin was done.

Chapter 2

AS RJ WAS lying there, he thought back to when he'd first started playing football. He liked to remember those early games, because they'd made him who he was today. He was just focused on the game, trying to make sure he was the best player there, the player that people talked about.

His home life had certainly never indicated that he'd be starting for a college team. His dad was a gym teacher at the local high school, and his mother was a writer. That combination of incomes made them just this side of poor. He never wanted for anything, though. Mom always found a freelance gig or a ghostwriting job when things were tight, so that they could make the bills. Dad didn't coach like most of the other gym teachers he knew. He just did his day job, then headed home for the evening. He was home with RJ in the summers and during the other breaks.

There was a lot of togetherness growing up. RJ remembered that the family would be home together all summer, since Dad was off and Mom was home most days. The times together had made them close, but there were still riffs in the family. Some of RJ's extended family didn't come around, which no one liked to talk about.

Their two-bedroom home in Old Saybrook, Connecticut was small but perfect for the three of them. It had a white picket fence in front, and a boxy façade that made it look like something out of the last century. The backyard was big enough for him to practice kicking a soccer ball or trying for the fence with a baseball. However, even at an early age, RJ preferred football. He wasn't sure if it was a natural talent or if others had pushed him toward the sport. He could remember watching college games with his Grandpa Robinson during the holidays. Every Thanksgiving and Christmas, they'd watch football and talk about the players and the games. His grandfather had an amazing memory for details of games that had happened long before RJ was even born.

RJ wanted to start playing when he was six, but his dad drew the line: He wasn't playing football that young. His father pulled out articles about children and concussions, young boys having their growth plates broken by bad falls. He'd been more adamant about telling him no than he had been about anything else. He'd insisted that RJ wait until he was nine to start. Some of the other kids had been playing for years, getting to know the teams around the area and building camaraderie with the other players.

RJ immediately felt that loss when he started. He'd missed out on three years of bonding with those guys, and they never let him forget it for a moment. He'd been an outsider then, and the drive to fit in was hard to resist. Lots of those boys hung out together after school, and went to the malls together on the weekends after the games. A few of the parents had boats and spent the weekends sailing. RJ had wished for a boat once, but his parents laughed and pointed out that they couldn't afford to be in the boat crowd.

Only once in a great while, RJ was invited to something, and only by a few of the guys. Most of the team either forgot him or didn't invite him on purpose. RJ spent his off-time debating which one would be worse: being ignored or forgotten. He never came up with a good answer to his question.

So he did the only thing he could do. RJ decided to be the best on the team. It wasn't enough to play. It wasn't enough to just do well. He had to outshine all the other players on the team. It was an idea that his grandfather had come up with, and it made sense to RJ, who wanted to fit in.

Grandpa Robinson had always been a huge supporter of RJ's, and he knew that he wouldn't have come this far without the old man's help. The hours of practice in the backyard had come from his grandpa, who showed him the best way to throw a pass, the fastest way to sack a quarterback, and the best way to punt. Grandpa had wanted RJ to excel in all the positions, not just quarterback, even though RJ had his eye on that position from the start. Only then could he possibly tell all those boys what to do.

Even back then, he'd recognized his own father's reticence toward the game. His dad occasionally showed up to the games, but more often than not, only Grandpa was there to cheer him on. Dad would find something else to occupy his time, something that didn't involve RJ. For a few years, his father had been involved with restoring cars. After that, it had been target shooting. He always had something to do on a Saturday afternoon. RJ couldn't understand it because his father had every Saturday free from school. PE teachers didn't really have any hours on Saturdays. But after so many years of absences, RJ had stopped asking where his father was.

His mother came to an occasional game, but for the most part, RJ found her typing furiously on weekends, trying to get another piece over to an editor so they could pay the bills. He admired her concentration and determination. She knew what her family had to do in order to get by, and she did it without complaining. She didn't feel sorry for herself, or wish for the day that her husband would take a better-paying job. If she wanted more, she wrote more.

He remembered one important conversation with his mother. He'd learned to live with her answer, even though it never satisfied him.

"Mama, why don't you and Dad come to my games?" he'd asked one afternoon. "All the other boys have parents there who watch them and cheer for them." He and his mom had baked some cookies to celebrate the football team's win over their biggest rival. RJ had played quarterback and thrown 300 yards during the game. The coaches had talked to Grandpa Robinson for a long time after the game, but none of them would tell him what they'd talked about. "It was grownup stuff," the men had said. RJ felt like a twelve-year-old again, listening to the adults talk.

His mom had walked over to him and given him a big hug. She smelled of sugar and whatever had been in the oven that day. He grabbed her around the waist and hugged her back.

"RJ, sweetie, that's not true. Many of the boys don't have family there. They get dropped off and picked up. So if all of us come and root you on, how do you think they're going to feel about it?" She stroked his hair softly as she spoke.

"Probably unhappy," RJ replied after some thought. "I guess I understand why you two don't come. Grandpa's enough of a fan himself."

His mom had laughed. "That he is, honey, that he is."

So RJ had gotten used to the Saturday routine. Grandpa Robinson would come and pick him up. They'd drive to the game, while talking about the plays for this game and the ways that RJ could make improvements over the previous game. Sometimes, he and Grandpa would take the field between games and throw the ball. Grandpa didn't believe in sitting on the bench and talking to the other guys, and that suited RJ just fine, since most of the other boys still didn't talk to him.

Over RJ's first two years of football, it became a tradition that he and Grandpa practiced out on the field before each game. Sometimes, other boys would join in, but mostly it was just the two of them. RJ was fine with that. Even though his grandpa talked to him like an adult, RJ was occasionally jealous of the ease that the players had when they joked with each other. He didn't have that kind of relationship with any of them.

The better game in town didn't involve being on another school's team, but being part of a local league. Grandpa Robinson had told him that nothing ever came from the school leagues, but that scouts sometimes came to the local league games. RJ was glad to hear that important people would see him play and enjoy the game. But at that time, he didn't really understand the importance of his grandfather's words.

RJ was well into his second season with the Old Saybrook Seagulls before he was noticed by anyone. The first season had been uneventful. Even his grandfather hadn't expected much, but RJ was given plenty of time on the field, which had made him happy.

Then halfway through the second season, they played a similar team out of Niantic. The Niantic team was known for recruiting youngsters from across New England to move into the area, so they could claim the yearly title in the league. RJ hadn't known any of this going into the game. He wasn't up on this league like he was with college and pro ball.

Of course, after he was able to play a few minutes in the first half, he quickly figured everything out. Defense stayed out on the field, holding the Niantic squad to only one touchdown. Still, RJ was fidgety. He wanted to play. All this sitting around was not for him. The line didn't hold, and during two plays, he'd been forced to throw the ball to prevent being sacked. RJ knew that his grandpa would have extra sprints and calisthenics for him to do if he was sacked.

In the first play of the second half, RJ watched as two of their best running plays netted them about ten inches toward the first down. He rolled his eyes. RJ wasn't used to being bested by another team. He looked around at the boys around him. He barely knew them, but he assumed that they weren't fond of it either.

Out on the field, RJ decided to switch signals and go for a long pass, even though they weren't supposed to. (The coach had said they weren't ready for it.) Tyler was going to run down the field, while two others faked out the Niantic team with short maneuvers near the first-down marker. RJ would fake a throw to one of the two, then pass to Tyler downfield.

The play worked just as RJ had called it. The Niantic team was faked out by the two players and focused on them, thinking that no one would pass for major yardage against them. Tyler caught the ball and ran it for a touchdown. The crowd went wild.

The coach was less than pleased by the play. He whooped, realizing that they were tied with the best team in the league. RJ grinned at the fulsome praise. However, the coach pulled RJ from the next quarter and made him sit out. RJ didn't understand why he was being punished for putting them on the board, but he knew that some people lived by strict rules. And violating them involved punishment.

But Grandpa Robinson didn't care about those rules. He snagged a copy of the play from someone filming the game, and it ended up on the nightly news. The story was picked up by stations as far as Boston. Not every ten-year-old can hit a receiver with a 53-yard pass, and tie the game against the best team around.

RJ thought the play would help cement his place on the team and net him some more invitations to parties and events with the other players, but it didn't. Unfortunately, RJ found that excellence made others suspicious. Now he was both an outsider on the team and a player to watch out for.

Chapter 3

BACK IN COLLEGE, the week had been uneventful, which RJ was grateful for. He was still a bit shocked at what Kevin had done the previous weekend.

RJ went to his classes, ate in the dining hall, and went to practice. Once again, he found himself very alone. While many of his teammates took Art Appreciation and Music Studies just to keep their GPAs up, RJ's parents insisted on a real education for their son. So he hadn't enrolled in any of the simplistic classes, which would allow you to graduate with a useless piece of paper. They'd all sat down and worked out a schedule that allowed him more time for sports in the fall, and more time for academics in the spring. RJ wasn't sure of a major yet, so most of the classes were the generic prerequisites that most freshmen had to take.

Even with the lighter schedule they'd picked out, RJ had an English class, a history survey, and a philosophy class.

He'd taken a few AP classes in high school, which allowed him to skip a few classes. To vary the workload, he filled the slots with less taxing classes. RJ found that none of the classes were difficult; RJ had taken his share of these classes in high school, and much of the work resembled the assignments there.

Even with the relatively light load, RJ's more difficult classes served as another wedge between him and the other players. Most of the first-string had been there for two or three years, so they were used to professors vaguely pressuring them about keeping their grades afloat ("above C level," as the joke went).

But the first-stringers made it clear that they weren't there to study. They were there to party and play football. RJ wasn't used to that mindset. He'd had to work for everything he'd received, and the thought of coasting now was just wrong to him. If his calculations were correct, he could coast after the age of 30. Now was not the time to rest on his laurels. He had to prove himself to an entirely new school, just as he had in high school.

Fortunately, he found a good place to study in the campus library—on the third floor in a quiet corner with a view of the quad. He spent a few evenings there every week, using the library computer to look up any topic that he didn't understand. It was easier than trying to find a place in his dorm to study.

Kevin usually had his music on in the room or a sock on the door handle. And RJ didn't want a repeat of that first Saturday night. One evening, RJ sat on the floor outside the room and read for his English class. When Kevin finally opened the door at midnight, RJ was shocked to see another teammate come out of the room, along with five girls. After that, RJ felt like he needed a shower. He had no desire to live that kind of life.

Of all the changes to his daily routine, RJ missed talking to Mya the most. She was his rock, and not having her around made things much more difficult. He wouldn't have called himself homesick, but he definitely missed her. They talked on the phone daily, sometimes for an hour or more, but it didn't replace the hours they spent together. His parents had splurged to buy him a phone with an unlimited plan, knowing that their son would not fare well without his girlfriend.

All of these things kept him busy, but RJ could already feel a growing chasm between himself and the other players. He'd really hoped that college would be different in this respect. He wanted to feel like he was part of the team, rather than a lone player tolerated for his superior skills. Yet he was now two weeks into school, and he felt the same way he had in junior high. He wondered if the trouble was with him, or if he just wasn't meant to fit in with the crowd.

Mya didn't particularly feel sorry for him. She was attending Three Rivers Community College, not far from where they'd grown up. She was getting a degree in technology. Then she'd have a career to fall back on if RJ didn't make it big. She was always practical, and never took a pro-football career for granted. Mya planned as though the NFL might never happen, and she was fine with that possibility.

Mya had to work two jobs while attending school, and the thought of his full ride to State made her more than a little envious. Like RJ, she always had to work for what she got, and college was no different for her. He wished there was a way for him to help her, but the scholarships didn't allow for any cash stipends.

That's not to say that he didn't have perks on campus. RJ found that he didn't even have to do his own laundry on campus. No all-night coin-operated nightmare for him. He put his clothes out, and they were returned cleaned and pressed in less than two days. Granted, the plan had originally been for uniforms, which might be seen on one of the many ESPN stations, but the laundry service took whatever was offered.

Even the benefits didn't make up for the fact that he was still an outsider. As the second Friday of the semester rolled around, RJ found himself eating dinner alone at the dining hall. He'd brought a book, because he already knew that the guys would be eating out somewhere. He didn't know—or maybe didn't want to know—where they got the money they spent so freely. RJ knew that a few of the guys had rich parents. They'd talked about their families and their parents during practices and in the locker room.

Still, he felt the divide between the other players and him. It was as though they'd entered some club that RJ wasn't allowed to enter. Maybe they were waiting to see if he was as good as his hype. He'd never worried about peer pressure this much. He'd actually been so popular in high school that others had emulated him. Now he was just one of many exceptional athletes who had to prove themselves, and he had to do it alone. It was an odd feeling to be at the bottom of the ladder again, and be expected to start again. He'd enjoyed those few years of being popular more than he cared to admit, especially now that he'd lost it.

That Saturday was the first home game of the season. So on Friday night, RJ went to bed early. In fact, he was asleep long before Kevin even got home. RJ wasn't really sure what time his roommate had come in, but at least he hadn't been asked to leave so Kevin could have a party in the room again. Perhaps even Kevin knew this was a big game for State.

RJ was up early. He always liked to have some time before a game to psych himself up. He did some pushups and got in a short run before taking a shower. However, even after the many games he'd played, RJ felt nervous. He could screw up or get hurt. So he knew how much was riding on each play.

It didn't make it any easier that the home opener was against Ann Arbor U, one of the nation's powerhouse football teams. He'd actually done a few campus trips there. But the distance from Mya would have been too much, so he'd declined their offer. He knew that he needed to see her at times, and the distance from Connecticut to Ann Arbor was too far. The coach had offered plane trips home to see his girlfriend, and had been rather upset that RJ had chosen another school. So he wondered if the coach for Ann Arbor would want to get revenge today.

Ann Arbor had a great team. They went to the Rose Bowl the year before, and all of their starters were now back as seniors—a year older, wiser, and stronger. Even during a normal year, they were an intimidating team, and they were better this year. RJ was going to have a tough game ahead of him.

Grandpa Robinson called early that morning, so they could run over the plays that Ann Arbor was likely to use. They lengthily discussed which strategies would best serve RJ's team, and would play to Ann Arbor's weaknesses. After the discussion, RJ felt better, knowing that at least he'd have an arsenal of plays to use. In a way, it felt like cramming for a test, but he was comfortable with it.

RJ remembered how often he'd done the same thing in his grandfather's car on the way to a game in middle school and high school. They'd review the other team's strengths and weaknesses. Grandpa always told him that you needed to know what an opponent did well, along with how to exploit what they did poorly.

"Grandpa, I have to tell you that I'm nervous about this."

Grandpa chuckled. "You'd be an idiot not to be. They're a tough team. The bright spot is that most of the betting pools are more worried about whether or not State will score today. You're going to win. I know it, Robert Junior." RJ sat down on the bed and waited for the lecture. Grandpa Robinson only used his full name when he was about to give a speech.

"You have a great gift. You're smart, and you're a natural at football. I know this is a big game, and you feel like you have to live up to your title. But I'll tell you what: You already have. You're starting for State in a huge game. I know you're going to do your best. You're ready for this. Just keep a level head, and you'll be fine."

"Thanks. I'm just feeling alone right now."

"Robert, I'll tell you: It's lonely at the top. Some of the team will be jealous of your abilities, and others are just used to the hierarchy of freshmen being ignored. You may be lonely at times, but you have me. You have Mya.

You have your parents. Don't let the little people bring you down."

Over the years, RJ had learned to just let his grandfather talk when he was in this mood, and try not to interrupt him. He waited for the lecture to end, and before they said goodbye, they talked about his parents for a little bit.

The game started a little after 1 pm that afternoon. The stadium was full, and it seated 75,000. The noise was deafening as fans stomped on the metal bleachers and shouted. Many of them were drunk and shouted obscenities as the rival team came onto the field.

RJ panicked at first, not used to the roar of a crowd. His high school games had brought in maybe 2,000 fans. He scanned the sea of fans and looked over at the bank of cameras. The press was out in full force today. RJ could see all the major networks, along with two ESPN stations and a few others. RJ was used to attention, but this was his national debut. RJ swallowed hard, knowing what was riding on this game.

The game started. RJ came out for his first play, and the stands went wild. The cheering was thundering to the point that the team had trouble hearing his calls. One of the receivers either misunderstood or hadn't heard the play, so he wasn't in the proper place for a pass. RJ quickly scanned the field, looking for an open receiver. He found one and hit him with the ball. The receiver made it to the first-down marker.

The success of the first play made RJ relax somewhat, but the next two plays didn't earn them any additional yardage. They had to punt, and RJ soon found himself on the sidelines, waiting for the defense to do its job.

"Not a bad pass out there, Robinson. But I like a QB who can think on his feet. What happened?" Coach leaned down so RJ could hear him. The crowd was still louder than anything he'd heard.

RJ explained that some of the team had not been able to hear the signals to execute the play. The coach nodded. "I thought it might have been something like that. You know you can use hand signals, right? They're more difficult to use, but they're better than not being heard at all." The coach went over a few hand signals with him. He stood up and walked away, watching the defense try to prevent Ann Arbor from getting a touchdown.

The defense was successful, but Ann Arbor opted to kick a field goal, which made the score 3-0.

When RJ returned to the field, he was more careful. He made sure that everyone knew their roles. He chose one of the plays that his grandfather had suggested that morning. In this game, RJ wanted to match Ann Arbor score-for-score. He didn't want to be playing catch-up in the fourth quarter. He had enough pressure as it was.

The team got into formation. This time around, RJ was satisfied that no one misunderstood the play. However, as soon as the ball snapped, he realized that both his team and Ann Arbor understood it. Almost as if they could read his mind, his teammates were covered by Ann Arbor players. RJ looked for an opening, but there wasn't one. As he tried to find an opening, he counted off the seconds in his head. But nothing opened up. They were covered. One of the linemen tried to break free, but an Ann Arbor player followed his every step.

With a grunt, one of the Ann Arbor players broke through the line, and RJ knew he had to act right away. His grandfather had repeatedly told him that real quarterbacks didn't get sacked, and he replayed that message in his head as he decided what to do. For one of the first times in his football career, RJ had to rely on his own instincts. He ran the ball.

RJ eluded the player who had been charging and ducked to the left, where two of his teammates were battling to hold back the Ann Arbor players. He didn't motion to them, since he didn't want to let them know that he still had the ball tucked under his arm. They didn't understand, but then neither did the Ann Arbor players, until he was a few yards past them.

Suddenly, it became a sprint downfield. RJ focused on his breathing and pace, and nothing else. He tuned out his coach, the crowd, and the knowledge that some very big, pissed men were on his tail. RJ had no idea what the coach would say about him running the ball, but so far, he'd made a first down, which was more than a sack at the line of scrimmage would have gotten him.

He continued his pace, and didn't let up—despite the heat, and despite the knowledge that he'd be exhausted after this play. Inside his helmet, sweat poured down his face as he ran. He didn't care, though. It had been the right play at that moment, and he didn't regret it.

The goal line was in sight now, coming up fast. RJ sprinted over the line, and the crowd went wild. He was aware of the crowd now, hearing the stomps and shouts of the thousands in the stands. But he didn't do any dancing or celebrating in the end zone. He merely tossed the ball to the referee, and slowly walked back to the sidelines.

The coach was waiting for him when he got back. "That was a dumbass play, but it worked. Later, we'll talk about how to make sure that the other team doesn't know what you're doing before you do it. Your call was too obvious. A youth football team could have guessed you would do that, which explains why they were ready for you." He handed RJ a bottle of Gatorade, sensing that he was worn out.

RJ finished the bottle before he spoke. "Thanks, Coach. I still have a lot to learn here."

Coach rolled his eyes. "Yeah, you do. But that was still a gutsy play, and the crowd loved it. I'm going to have you sit out a quarter and rest up. Then you'll play again, just before the half. I want to have the crowd wound up before we go to halftime."

RJ nodded and looked over at the cameras rolling. Ratings were important to the school, which relied on football money to support some of their other programs. He'd never considered a TV audience before. Now he wondered how that last play would look on-screen.

RJ took a seat on the bench next to Kevin, who was suited up but not wearing a helmet. His roommate gave him a smile. "Nice play, show-boater. I didn't think you had it in you, all quiet and studious. I might have to rethink you." He laughed at his last sentence, but RJ wasn't sure what was so funny about what he'd said. What impression did his roommate have of him? RJ's mind left the game for a few minutes, as he tried to determine what that might mean.

He returned his attention to the game when the second-string quarterback went into play. There was some booing in the stands, and RJ winced. He was glad to be liked by the fans, but winning the game was more important than any single player. He knew that, and he hoped the fans knew it, too. They wouldn't want to spook the second-string man, who might screw up the play if he was too focused on their negative behaviors.

True to his word, Coach put RJ back in at the end of the second quarter. The score hadn't budged since he'd left the game: It was still 7-3. With only a few minutes left on the board, RJ tried to pass downfield and get the down before time ran out. He hit three passes in a row to the receiver he wanted. The crowd was excited, but to RJ, it felt rote. He wanted another show-stopping play, but they were once in a season—if not once in a lifetime.

The clock ran out, and the team trudged back to the locker room. The guys managed to cool off in various ways, from dumping ice down their shirts to gulping water. It was a scorcher that day, even if you were just resting in the shade. The room was ripe, but no one made a move to take a shower.

Coach called them all together and gave them a pep talk. He didn't have to say much. The expectations for a win all rested with Ann Arbor, not with State. But they were winning. They could just play their best damn game, and it would be more than enough. Coach was excited because he knew that RJ's play in this game would be the talk of the sports shows that weekend. He'd get some interviews out of it, and they'd likely raise a lot of money from the alumni and boosters. RJ guessed that the school had probably netted a cool million dollars from that play alone.

They went back out onto the field. The crowd was somehow even more revved up than before. The noise level made it difficult to hear the other players. The second half went against State. Ann Arbor regained their confidence during halftime, and the first drive down the field resulted in a touchdown.

But it turned out that RJ really only had one big play that day. Due to Ann Arbor's defense, most of his downs were short of the yardage needed. They blocked too well and hit too hard for State to overcome their advantage. It was mostly three plays, then punt.

Even so, the score at the end of the game was 10-7, which was far better than anyone would have predicted. RJ took a shower after the game. He had nowhere to be, and no one to meet. So he took his time. Many of the players had already left by the time he grabbed his bag to leave. He walked slowly out of the locker room, still going over the game in his mind.

Just outside the doors, the press mobbed him. RJ saw Kevin leave without so much as a request for a quote. But he knew that the quarterback usually got credit for a game, even when the whole team contributed. RJ answered questions over and over, providing the same platitudes that all players gave to reporters. He grew tired of spouting the same ideas in different words.

As the press began to dissipate, he heard a familiar voice. He looked up to see that Mya was there. He grabbed her and swung her around. He was so happy to see her that he forgot his aches and pains for a few minutes. "What are you doing here, baby? I didn't expect to see you."

She kissed him on the mouth, letting her lips linger against his. He slid his tongue between her lips and found her tongue. They spent a few minutes just kissing. The hunger of not seeing each other for weeks showed. A few cameras caught them as they kissed, but he didn't care. He loved this girl with all of his heart.

Mya finally broke away. "Well, I wasn't sure if you'd be glad to see me or not," she laughed. "But I can tell I don't have to worry about that."

He lifted her up and squeezed her tightly, then easily placed her back down on the ground. "I'm just surprised. I thought you'd watch the game on TV."

She shook her head. "The debut of the sexiest quarterback ever to come out of Old Saybrook? I wouldn't miss that for the world. And I got a student ticket for cheap. You wouldn't believe the traffic, though. All coming to see my baby." She gave him a squeeze. "And I'm the lucky one. I get to go home with him tonight."

RJ gave a laugh. This was exactly what he'd needed. Mya could always bring him out of his thoughts long enough to enjoy life. He tended to be too intense and stressed without her. He scraped together the money to take her into town for a meal. Then they went back to his dorm room, where RJ was finally the one putting the sock on the door handle.

Chapter 4

LATER THAT NIGHT, as RJ was holding Mya in his arms, he remembered how they'd first met. It seemed hard to believe that they'd known each other nearly seven years, and in all that time, they'd never fought or cheated. Their longevity was a record in his group of friends from school, which first began in the youth football team he'd played for in middle school.

Grandpa Robinson had decided that RJ should play in a youth league. He made this decision after RJ learned that the school team already had a starting quarterback. No amount of talent would ever dislodge him as the starter, since he happened to be the coach's son. Grandpa was not happy with that situation, even using a number of words that RJ had never heard from him before.

RJ spent two weeks in the Youth Football League that summer, practicing his skills. Grandpa wanted him to be at peak performance for the start of the season.

Grandpa was friends with one of the coaches in the league, who had been anxious to see RJ in action. The coach was impressed, and RJ started for the team three weeks later. RJ knew his grandfather would be pleased. The coach pushed the existing quarterback to second-string, but the boy didn't seem to mind. He just sat on the bench and talked to his friends, not really noticing the game going on.

RJ liked the league, but his family's choice isolated him from his classmates. He was the only player from his middle school, so most of the other players didn't know him or have much in common with him. Once again, he didn't get many invitations to events or parties. They lived in the suburbs or the next town over, so visits were more trouble than they were worth to his parents.

Yet, in the midst of all that isolation, he met Mya. He was sitting out during the fourth quarter of a game, since he'd already won it for the team. She was in the stands, and she immediately caught his eye.

She had dark hair, dark eyes, and skin the color of chocolate. She was shy about her smile, but when she gave it to him, he wanted to melt. And she had an easy laugh when she talked to her family. On one occasion, RJ wanted to talk to her so much that he actually thought about throwing an interception, just to go back to the bench again.

It turned out that she was the cousin of one of RJ's teammates, the only other African American on the team. Matt and RJ didn't have much in common besides their race, so they didn't become friends. However, Matt was more than willing to introduce them.

"Mya, this poor dude thinks you're cute. I keep telling him differently, but he won't listen." Matt laughed at his own joke, and ducked Mya's hand as she tried to swat him upside the head. They seemed to be on good terms, and Mya turned her attention to RJ.

RJ flushed, feeling like everyone could see how embarrassed he was. He hadn't really talked to many girls that he liked. Mostly, he talked to them about football until their eyes glazed over, and they left without looking back. Since he didn't play for his middle school, he lacked the reputation that would have made him a catch. There, he was just another student who had trouble talking to girls.

Mya was different, though. She liked football. In fact, she'd given him some pointers on his game. She talked to him about relying more on running than passing, and she pointed out some of the weaknesses of the other teams in the league. She was definitely his type of girlfriend.

His parents were less enthusiastic about the match. His mother felt outnumbered, due to the amount of sports discussed. She explained her lackluster welcome with this excuse: RJ was an only child, and she'd always hoped for a daughter who was prissy and into dresses and other girly things. Mya was definitely not like that.

For some reason, his father wanted a girl who would rather gossip than talk about gridiron. Dad wasn't much for talking sports at all, much less with a girl who was dating his son.

Only Grandpa Robinson was happy about RJ's romantic interest. In fact, he occasionally slipped RJ a few bills so he could take Mya out to dinner. He was just happy to have another person to talk football with.

The relationship slowly progressed. Mya lived too far away for frequent visits. Since RJ depended on his parents, who didn't approve, he had to wait for the Saturday games and other events to see her. Real dates were few and far between, usually with one of his parents chaperoning the whole time. The big sex talk in junior high had been for nothing, since he and Mya were never left alone long enough to do anything.

Like most parents, RJ's parents forgot what it was like to be young: Their response only made RJ more determined to see Mya as much as he could. He talked his grandfather into going to games earlier. Then he could sit and talk to her in the stands until his game started. She talked Matt's family into staying after the game, so that they could hang out longer. Once in a while, she even visited Matt's house, so they could have time together.

However, Matt's mom watched Mya almost as closely as she watched her son.

RJ eventually managed to find a place where they could talk and kiss in private while they were watching games. The path to the food vendors took two curves up the hill, and once past that first curve, there was a small grouping of lush trees and bushes. Long ago, someone had placed two benches in the middle of the trees, and you could go there and talk without being seen.

Of course, they couldn't be gone for long, or else people would come looking for them. Still, it was their place, and during the Saturday games, they went there as often as they could.

The end of the Youth Football League season came too soon for RJ. He'd managed to keep his head in the game. He'd even set a record for most yards passed that season. His name was in the newspapers, and Grandpa Robinson pulled some strings to get him featured on a local TV station. By then, his middle school had taken notice of him, but it was too late. He was committed to the YFL, especially since it included seeing Mya on a regular basis.

However, winning the YFL Championship in November meant that he would no longer see Mya every week. And he knew that it was going to be months before there were any practices for the league. He traced the route to her house on a map, but it was ten miles one way. RJ knew he'd never get away with a trip that long by foot, even if he ran.

Despite his parents' objections, Grandpa Robinson bought him a cellphone after the season was over. At least if he couldn't see her, he could still talk to her.

Chapter 5

BACK IN THE present, RJ had a newfound popularity on campus after Mya left on Sunday morning. His strategy in the Ann Arbor game was being called "the play" in the local papers. It had been a hit on cable sports stations, where it had repeatedly aired for almost 48 hours straight. By the time Monday rolled around, everyone at State had heard about it.

RJ was surprised when even his English professor mentioned it during class on Monday. Then he'd been mobbed by some students in the quad, who wanted an autograph or a photo with him. He'd even had one girl request that he autograph her chest, but he demurred. The time with Mya had grounded him in his goals, and his path to get there.

On Wednesday after the game, RJ rediscovered the LeBron X's that had been waiting for him on his first day there. He still hadn't done anything with the shoes, and he wanted to resolve the situation. "Kevin, who gave me these shoes?" RJ asked again, hoping to get a better answer now that he'd proven his worth to the team.

Kevin shrugged. He was resting on his bed, listening to his iPod again. RJ had yet to see him crack open a book since he'd been here. He didn't know what Kevin did with all his spare time. "Don't know. Don't care. They're some sweet kicks. Why would you want to know where they came from?"

RJ frowned. "I want to return them. I don't want to be bought for a pair of shoes. I plan on being my own man here."

Kevin laughed at his roommate. "Yeah, I give it four months before you have your hand out like everyone else around here. You probably made this school a cool million last weekend. Coach was paid for his interviews. Based on your performance, the school got donations and grants. Let me ask you: How much did you get paid for that play?"

RJ didn't want to argue this point. He'd heard it all before. Everyone else cashed in on NCAA money, so why shouldn't the players? He'd heard the stories of players who eked out their scholarship funds to get by, but who couldn't buy a can of soda because they were so broke. RJ wasn't going to be quite that bad, because he could rely on his grandfather. But he was definitely in the broke category.

He knew that the system wasn't fair. It needed an overhaul, but RJ wasn't there to reset the axis of the world. He was there to win games and be a draft pick, at least by the third round. Then he'd have his chance at real money, so he could sweat it out for three more years. At that point, he'd only need a few seasons in the NFL before he'd be set.

RJ tried not to show his emotions to his roommate. He didn't want Kevin to know that thinking about the money had gotten to him. "You know what I got for that play. So who gave me the LeBron's?"

Kevin sighed. "Not going to argue with a goody two-shoes. Edward Donley gave them to all the players, including freshmen. It's a kind of a welcome-to-school gift. He does this every year. No big deal."

RJ nodded. He'd heard the name before. Donley was a booster of the highest order. He'd somehow made his money in the tech market, and now he spent millions supporting his alma mater, especially in sports. RJ put the shoes in a box, wrapped the package in brown paper, and wrote Donley's name on the outside.

"I'm going to drop these off with Coach," RJ said. "You want me to take yours, too?"

Kevin laughed again. "You're funny. First, I don't give back what I'm given, and second, I sold mine on eBay last week. How do you think I can afford to party on my parents' salaries?"

RJ took the box and went to Coach's office, which was located in the building on the side of the main stadium. Coach actually had two offices available to him: A small one for private phone calls just outside the locker rooms in the stadium, and the more luxurious one that RJ was currently in.

The outer room of the second office had leather chairs, thick carpeting, and a large wooden desk for his secretary. RJ hadn't been there since he was interviewing schools. At the time, it had seemed welcoming. Now it just seemed imposing.

"You're RJ Robinson, aren't you? I saw you at the game on Saturday," the secretary said with a broad grin. "May I help you?"

RJ explained why he was there. The woman raised an eyebrow when he said he wanted to return the shoes.

"I'm not sure how that would work," she replied. "I've never had to do this before. Is it because they don't fit, or you don't like the color? We can always replace them if you'd like."

RJ explained that he didn't want to be caught breaking the rules. He talked about the East Orange U scandal: Boosters gave gifts to the players, who were later suspended for accepting them.

The secretary reluctantly took the shoes and put them on the edge of her desk. RJ left, feeling better for having resolved the issue.

At least, RJ thought it was resolved until that Friday.

Then another pair of shoes showed up in RJ's room. They were identical to the ones he'd dropped off two days earlier, except this pair was dark blue. He shook his head. Apparently, college ethics were going to be more difficult than he'd thought.

But Kevin just laughed when he saw the new LeBron's. He took them from the box and laced them up. He threatened to hold RJ down and shove them on his feet unless he at least tried them on. "You don't know what you're missing. They are fine."

RJ took a shoe and tried it on. The shoes were light. It was like he was walking on air as he walked around the room. At the bottom of the box, there was a note from the Athletic Director. It said that funds for the shoes had been donated to the athletic department by Edward Donley, but that the Athletic Director was at liberty about how best to allocate them. And he deemed the shoes a necessity for athletes.

Knowing it was just an elaborate farce to get around the rules, RJ looked down at the shoes. He suspected that pushing this situation any further would only get the department and the coach mad at him. He didn't want to rock the boat too much, given that he was there on a full ride. At this point, others were in charge of his future. In order to stay, he had to perform—and perform well. RJ resented that he had such a limited part in what happened to him here. He was used to taking responsibility for himself.

He didn't like the feeling. While he'd always put pressure on himself to do his best, he'd also known that school was a separate entity; the two were not dependent on each other in any way. He felt scrutinized as he tried to imagine what would happen to his education if he pushed too hard about an issue like the shoes. He didn't want to take the chance of angering anyone until he was sure that he could prove himself to the school.

Even with his increased popularity, RJ found himself eating alone in the dining hall that night. The other guys from the team had gone out for pizza in town. RJ pondered selling the shoes, like Kevin had done. But given his earlier protest, he didn't know what the coaches would say if he didn't return them now. It was a risk he didn't want to take.

RJ went home right away and studied his philosophy text, since he had a test on Monday. Then he went to bed early to get rested for their second home game the next day.

About midnight, Kevin returned to the room. And true to form, he had some girls with him. (RJ had tried to explain to Mya what a freak his roommate was, but he wasn't sure that she believed him.) Kevin and the girls whispered and giggled as they undressed. RJ pretended to stay asleep as his roommate went another round with two women.

He wasn't sure what Kevin's deal was with multiple partners. Perhaps he didn't want to have an emotional involvement. And a girl definitely wouldn't think she was his one and only if she wasn't even his only one that night. He just hoped that Kevin was being safe. If all these girls got pregnant, he'd have enough kids to start his own team.

At some point, RJ went back to sleep. When he woke up again, sunlight was streaming in the window, and Kevin was alone in his bed.

RJ got up, showered, went to breakfast, and came back to his room to call Grandpa Robinson. Since Grandpa's plays hadn't worked with Ann Arbor, RJ was hesitant about this week's talk. Usually, he found the talks to be reassuring. But if the other team already knew all the plays that Grandpa was suggesting, then the conversations had lost one of their major benefits. So RJ decided to continue the talks, but follow Coach's suggestions instead. If he could, RJ would include a play that his grandfather recommended as an offering to his elders. But after that last game, he knew he had to follow Coach's directions first, and only follow his grandfather's suggestions if time permitted.

Grandpa picked up on the second ring. "RJ, I just sent you links to a few videos. Go check your email."

RJ was always amazed at how tech-savvy his grandfather was. Some of his professors were a decade younger than Grandpa Robinson, and barely knew how to send an email. But Grandpa scoured YouTube, Skype, Facebook, and Twitter for videos of other teams.

RJ signed into his email, and clicked on the first link.

"Take a look at this. I watched the first two games that East Coast State played this season. They struggled with two defensive plays. The first is a quick-hit play. Go to an hour and 25 minutes into the video."

RJ dragged the pointer to that time, and watched as a quick-hit play unfolded. Sure enough, East Coast State had a more patient defense, waiting until the ball was passed off to move. "After last week, they'll be expecting you to do the same play. They're going to expect misdirection and fakes. And they'll wait to move until they know who really has the ball. If you do some fast plays like this, you'll totally confuse them."

They went through a number of other plays that East Coast State seemed to have trouble with, until RJ said that he had to go. They hung up, and RJ decided to go to the coach with his grandfather's ideas. In one way, he felt like a traitor, questioning what his grandfather had told him. The man had been his advisor for years. But he didn't want to muff a play like he almost had last week. He wanted a smoother game. And since East Coast wasn't the powerhouse that Ann Arbor was, many expected State to win this game. In other words, RJ wanted this game to be his first win of the season.

RJ found the coach reading some materials at his desk in the office near the locker room of the stadium.

"Ready to run 'the play' again?" Coach asked with a laugh. The joke was that it was a play that could not likely be repeated. In part, everyone would be expecting RJ to do it again, since it had garnered so much attention. Secondly, "the play" was stunningly difficult to pull off, which was why it had been so widely publicized.

RJ just smiled and shook his head. "I was talking with my grandpa about the plays for East Coast State, and he pointed out a few things that I wanted to run by you."

RJ repeated the difficulties that Grandpa had shown East Coast having with the quick-hit plays, especially since RJ would be expected to try that play again.

Coach almost immediately nixed the plays. "Listen, kid, I know you love your grandpa, but this is college. You can't let every armchair quarterback tell you what to do. It needs to be done the way we practiced." Coach specifically outlined what he expected RJ to do on the field during the game. In a minor nod to Grandpa,

Coach did allow them to try one fake run, followed by a quick hit. But only one.

This week, the game felt more comfortable. The crowd still numbered in the tens of thousands, but it didn't have as many cameras as the Ann Arbor game. When RJ saw that only a few cameras were on the sidelines, he felt something almost like relief. In fact, he felt like he could really focus without the pressure of every play being broadcast to millions of cable viewers.

By halftime, RJ had to admit that Coach was right. If he'd run a number of quick-hit plays, East Coast's defense would have annihilated him. They were expecting the unexpected, rather than waiting for yet another quarterback run to the goal. The defense had apparently been schooled to keep their eyes peeled for a unique play.

So instead, RJ stuck to his strengths: passes and short runs. He wished he could give the crowd (especially his grandpa) the big plays they obviously wanted, but he also knew they'd react well if he won the game.

By the half, State was up 17-7.

With a good lead, Coach let the second-string quarterback play the third quarter. RJ watched as the junior played a fairly routine game. He did nothing showy, and nothing that lost points. They ended the quarter with the same score.

During the fourth quarter, RJ went back in. Time was running out, but State still held its comfortable lead. Then RJ threw a short pass to a senior on the team, who fumbled the ball. Then it bounced, and practically landed in RJ's arms. Seeing too many orange jerseys headed his way, he knew that another outstanding play was out of the question. So he grabbed the ball with both hands, and started another run.

RJ did manage to get the ball to the first-down line, before he ran out of bounds. He wasn't going to get sacked by a team this late in the game. It wouldn't be worth it. Grandpa had always told him to stay away from the sack. A quarterback could be injured for life if he was hit too hard. Grandpa never called the quarterbacks weaker or less able to take a hit, but the words were left lingering in the air. A good quarterback had to be protected from the injuries and impacts that the rest of the team took for granted.

Even so, the crowd went wild after RJ's run. The play had been impromptu, and much shorter than last week's. But the fans still loved it. RJ hoped they wouldn't expect this every week. Soon, the other teams would be expecting him to run the ball himself, and the chance of injury would skyrocket. Then every team would have a price on RJ's head.

RJ knew that he'd be on the news cycle again this week—remembering the play from last week, and adding in the information about the seven-yard run today.

The clock ran out before any more film-worthy plays could be set up, but the stands went wild for the win. The team and Coach shouted and whooped as they made their way to the locker room. RJ took a long shower to ease his mind after the game. He was glad they'd won. Each win would make it easier for him when the time came to play in the NFL.

Grandpa talked about going pro early, but RJ wasn't sure. He didn't want to lose out on his education. He knew that a bad injury could sideline or end his career, and he didn't want to go back to college after being a pro. It was hard enough for him being just another student now. He couldn't imagine what the ridicule would be like after playing in the big time.

Grandpa was waiting outside the locker room, and smiled as RJ came out into the warm afternoon sun. He stuck out a hand to shake, then decided to give RJ a hug instead.

"Good job today. It's a pity that you didn't do more of the plays we talked about, but it worked well when you used them."

RJ was shocked to see him. Grandpa hadn't mentioned coming down today. With his arthritis and other health problems, the drive was hard on him. He could barely walk across the room, yet here he was.

"I caught a ride down with a friend today. He was coming this way, so he offered to take me with him." Grandpa mentioned a name, but it meant nothing to RJ. From his years of involvement in local sports, Grandpa had lots of friends, so it could have been any one of them. He shrugged it off as a well-timed coincidence.

He gave his grandfather a tour of the stadium and locker room. No one was still there. The stands were silent, so the hallways underneath the structure echoed as they walked to the locker room. RJ could practically feel the approval radiate from his grandfather.

"That's everything, unless you want to see my dorm room," RJ said as they came back outside.

"Is it as messy as your room at home? If so, I think I'll just save that for another day. Besides, my ride said that he'd be here at 4:30, and it's nearly that now."

As if on cue, a new black Lincoln Town Car pulled up to the stadium and blew its horn. RJ raised an eyebrow. He wasn't aware of any of Grandpa's friends being able to afford a luxury car. Most of them were working stiffs, like his family was. The man stepped out of the car, and waved at RJ. "You must be RJ. Your grandfather told me all about you. Great game today, by the way."

RJ nodded and said, "Thanks."

He hugged his grandfather, who got in the car and drove off.

RJ silently walked back to the dorm. He was glad for the time alone that day. Mya hadn't been able to make the game, since she had to work. "Someone needs to pay for my next semester," she'd pointed out to him. RJ wished he could help her out with bills, but at this point, all he had were his scholarships and grants. No hard cash.

When he got back to his room, he called home. "Mom, did you see the game?"

His mother laughed. "No, sweetie, a rerun of *Three's Company* was on, and we decided to watch it instead. Of course we watched it. You were wonderful."

RJ always enjoyed the way his mother refused to use any sports terms to describe his performance. She was always saying "wonderful" or "great." For a woman who made her living with words, she willfully neglected to learn sports talk. "Thanks. What's going on with you? How's Dad?"

"Your father is fine, and he loved that run after the fumble. I received some great news this week. I have a new freelance assignment, so we might be able to attend a few games now. It will take up most of my time, but the pay is fantastic. I had my agent go over the contracts, because it seemed too good to be true."

His mother explained that she'd been contacted to write a book on gardening, one of her favorite hobbies. The publisher, Osmond Books, had offered her more money than she'd ever made on a gig before, and she was excited about the opportunity. The money would allow her the time and funds to work on some of her own projects. RJ knew that his mother wanted to write a novel, but the demands of freelancing kept her from having enough time to fulfill her own dreams.

The company's name sounded familiar to RJ, but he let it go. He was glad to hear that things were going well for his parents. He knew they'd sacrificed a lot just to get him here, and he occasionally felt guilty that they couldn't enjoy themselves, because of their debts.

"I think we might be able to make it to the game in three weeks. I should have enough of a paycheck by then to afford the trip. We might even stay in a hotel for one or two nights."

She sounded almost giddy with the idea of staying away from home, even for a short trip. RJ wondered, *When was the last time my parents went away, just the two of them?* It had to have been a while. He felt the burden of doing well in college, so that they would eventually relax and be able to enjoy life more.

RJ chatted a bit more, then hung up to go eat dinner. The dining hall was nearly empty, as it usually was on Saturday evenings. Too many students were either out on the town with friends or eating with their visiting parents. He got some nods and a few high-fives for the game, but overall, most of the students left him alone. They probably assumed that he had enough friends on the football team, so they didn't offer to share their tables with him. They figured he could sit with anyone he wanted.

He sat by himself, glad that he'd brought a book to study. That way, it didn't make him appear too lonely, and he needed to keep up with his classes. English was becoming a bigger problem than he'd imagined. The teaching assistant for the class wanted a paper every week. Not a two or three-page report like they'd done in high school, but 5,000 words every week. RJ found the word count to be daunting, since it took him about one hour for every 500 words. But there was no rush like there was in sports. It was just long hours of drudgery.

He went back to the dorm, which was mercifully quiet that night. He began on a paper, but soon found his mind wandering. The events after the game kept coming back to him. To satisfy himself, he pulled up the webpage for Osmond Publishing, and soon discovered why it sounded so familiar. When he clicked on the Board of Directors page, there was Edward Donley—the booster who'd sent him the shoes.

Of course, the whole thing could have been a coincidence, but RJ really didn't believe in these kinds of random happenings. It was all connected, and he knew why: Donley was the biggest booster at the school, and he wanted to make sure that RJ didn't need to drop out due to lack of funds. If he couldn't give money directly to the quarterback, then he'd give money to RJ's family through another corporation.

RJ quickly googled the man who'd given his grandfather a ride that afternoon. Sure enough, the man was listed as an employee of Donley Paper, another subsidiary of Edward Donley's money. Damn, he wanted to stay away from the money and the boosters and the temptations. But now his family members were up to their ears in it. Did they know what they were taking on?

RJ suspected that his mother had no clue who was behind the offer. She would never have taken it if she did. His mother was a proud woman, and she would never have stooped to making money off her son's reputation. She wanted her writing to be read for its own merit. RJ debated the merits of telling his mother about the connection, but decided against it. Technically, she was providing work for the company, and he knew that she would write the very best book she could. There'd be no way for the NCAA to accuse her of receiving payment without working for it.

However, RJ had to wonder about his grandfather, who enjoyed the perks of being related to a star quarterback. He remembered that Grandpa would get compensated for the price of the tickets and parking for some of RJ's games. And he had no qualms about taking the freebies being offered. So he would be more of a worry than his mother.

RJ wondered if his grandfather knew about the connection here. The cost of the car ride was minimal, but it would be enough to get him suspended or thrown off the team—if it appeared that RJ was in the car. He felt a bit queasy, thinking about the ramifications of the whole thing.

RJ decided to postpone any discussions with his family. He wanted to talk to Coach first. RJ had come to trust his coach's opinions about these matters. He was sure that Coach had to know about these things. How could Coach justify it? Maybe Donley was skating just inside the lines of what was legal, and what would raise the eyebrows of the NCAA. RJ certainly hoped so.

He finally began working on his paper, wishing that words came as easily to him as they did to his mother. Then he'd already be done with this stupid paper. By the time he printed out the final copy of the paper, it was after 1 am, so he went to bed.

However, it was a long time before he was able to get to sleep. The images of gifts—and the proximity of a lifestyle that would provide for all of them—kept playing around the edges of his mind. He resolved to keep away from these temptations, but he knew how hard that would be.

Even with something as small as the LeBron's or a car ride, the temptation was there to ignore his ethics. The idea of rejecting a huge cash offer was easier to deal with, since it was so blatantly wrong. But the small perks were the ones he needed to watch—anything that landed in the gray area. He dozed off, still wondering how best to say no without hurting anyone's feelings, or hurting his chances of making it into the NFL.

Chapter 6

RJ HAD BEEN happy to finally hit high school. After a long talk (more like an argument), his grandfather relented and allowed him to play for his high school team. Grandpa had wanted him to continue at the all-boys Catholic high school, arguing that he had a better chance of being scouted in an elite school with a nationally known football team. He wanted the best for RJ, and he wanted the world to know how good he was at football.

On the other hand, RJ wanted a more normal life. He knew that schools looked at guys who were well-rounded, who were more than just jocks. So he'd planned to get involved in a few extracurricular activities, in order to complete his college application forms. He couldn't do that with the practice schedule for the Catholic school, which seemed to dominate every minute of his after-school time year-round.

Of course, it didn't hurt that Mya went to the public high school that RJ wanted to attend. They'd been seeing more of each other during football season, since she came to every game and many of the practices. And they also made up excuses to go to the mall or to a friend's house, where they could meet.

His parents finally resigned themselves to the fact that RJ was in love with her. It had taken nearly two years before they called her by name, and actually invited her to dinner. Of course, it all came with a price. He had to endure a second sex talk with his parents—warning him about premarital sex and the dangers of pregnancy. Even with that cringe-worthy moment, he was still glad that his parents had begun to accept her.

After his freshman year of high school, RJ finally talked his grandfather into letting him go to the local school. He knew that the Catholic school had a better football program, but in terms of loneliness, RJ was about at the end of his rope. He'd missed his freshman year of high school with Mya, so once again, he felt like an outsider as he entered his neighborhood school in 10th grade. Luckily, he'd made friends quickly, mostly through Mya, and he loved that he could now participate more fully in school.

RJ's anonymity ended during his first football game at the public school. He'd been named the second-string quarterback, since Jerry Sears (the starter) had been at the school the previous year. During the fourth quarter, RJ was put in after it looked like their team was definitely headed for a loss. The score was 34-10. RJ threw for nearly 200 yards of passing and another 85 in running. They hadn't won the game, but the fourth quarter was all in RJ's favor.

The following Monday, he was promoted to first-string, so Jerry lost his position as starter. He felt bad for the guy, but at the same time, he wanted to be scouted, and no one scouted second-string players.

At first, the game was viewed as a fluke—as if RJ had just had a good quarter. But as the season progressed, the entire school had to admit that he was the real deal. Ever the promoter, Grandpa Robinson had gotten him interviews with the sports anchors on the local news stations. He was player of the week twice that season.

RJ was thrilled to receive the accolades at school. For years, he'd been a standout player, but since he played in an outside league, no one at school had ever heard of him. RJ knew that he wasn't in the game just for the spotlight, but it was nice to actually receive those honors for once. Nevertheless, Mya made sure that his head didn't get too big.

After that first season, RJ enjoyed the fact that the people he had classes with still remembered who he was. He'd lost his anonymity, and the isolated feelings that he'd harbored for so long. Soon, he got involved with the debate team. The basketball coach had encouraged him to go out for the team, but RJ had promised his grandfather that he was a one-sport student. His grandfather was worried that playing other sports could lead to injuries that would sideline RJ for the following football season.

The biggest benefit was being with Mya every day. In middle school, every date with her had been a luxury, but now he could see her whenever he wanted. They planned their schedules to have the maximum number of classes together. They opted for the same afterschool activities. Their time together brought them closer. RJ theorized that his parents had secretly hoped that all of their time together would drive them apart, but it didn't.

During that first winter of school together, RJ and Mya decided to make love for the first time. In all the time they'd spent together through middle school, they'd never had a moment alone. They were either at a football field or being chauffeured by parents. It wasn't until RJ finally had his driver's license that they were finally able to find time alone.

RJ was incredibly nervous. Sure, he'd heard the stories from the locker rooms and the football players, but he'd never so much as seen a naked woman, outside of an occasional HBO movie. Her form was as foreign to him as playing baseball. He wanted everything to be perfect—a memory that they could share for the rest of their lives.

Of course, plans never match reality. RJ had opted to drive to an away game toward the end of his sophomore season. The game was three hours away, and the team booked a hotel for the night. Mya had told her parents that she was spending the night at a friend's house. The friend had agreed to forward all calls to Mya's phone, so she wouldn't get busted by her parents. Still, both of them were concerned about getting caught.

After dinner with the team, RJ managed to go back to his room without much of a problem. The other boys in the room had crashed out in another room for the night, not telling the coach. Mya had been waiting for him at the mall, and together they rode the three hours, talking and laughing. When they arrived at the hotel, RJ had checked in and signaled to Mya, so they could climb the stairs to the room. Their plan had gone well. They found the silence and the solitary environment to be different. They rarely had time alone. RJ had brought flowers, which were on the end table. They'd kissed and slowly stripped, enjoying the time when they could be undressed together. They had just gotten under the covers when the fire alarm sounded. The bells and sirens were so loud that they had no choice but to leave the room.

They stood outside half-dressed as the building emptied. A few players from the team saw RJ and Mya there. Mya knew that there would be trouble if the coach saw her, so she crept off to stand behind some family, pretending to be with them. She ducked down so that her head wasn't visible over the heads of the parents.

The coach found the team and did a quick headcount. Watching from a distance, RJ cringed when Coach couldn't find one of his most valuable team players. RJ watched as the older man wandered around the lot, looking for him. Coach had come within about ten feet of Mya when he stopped and motioned to RJ. In the darkness, Coach hadn't spotted her. He and the missing player reluctantly rejoined the group.

The jokes after that had made RJ blush. He had wanted a romantic evening, and instead, he'd gotten some third-rate sex comedy. After the alarm was cleared, they went back to the room.

When they'd returned home, Mya's parents had found out about the tryst, and she was grounded for nearly a month. She'd somehow kept her phone, and their only communication after their night of romance was limited to text messages and secret phone calls.

RJ had vowed that he wouldn't do that again, since it cost them too much time together. However, he'd been surprised that Mya had soon wanted to do it again. She was not a shy lover. She was very direct, just like she was in everything else in her life. They'd found times together and made the most of it.

The word of their heightened relationship created a certain status at the high school. RJ continued to win football games, but Mya was struggling. Her grades were good but not great, which likely meant a community college, rather than one of the universities that were likely to scout RJ.

After the years of feeling disenfranchised, RJ secretly enjoyed being treated like royalty at school. He'd gone from being an unknown to being known by everyone. As a result, he and Mya were the junior prom king and queen, and the rumor was that they were a guaranteed favorite for the senior prom as well.

RJ's senior year was everything that he'd hoped it would be. During that stellar season, RJ made several personal and school records for passing, running, and games played, and the team went to the city tournament and the state tournament as well. Scouts had been to every game, sometimes filling several rows of the stadium in their desire to see RJ play.

And RJ didn't let them down. He was consistently a 20-point scorer for his team in running, passing, or both. The scouts interviewed during and after the games said they'd rarely seen such a mature player at the high school level.

He had offers from all over the country, but he had wanted to stay relatively close to home. So the California schools were scratched.

RJ enjoyed a relatively color-blind life, and his mother had encouraged him to stay out of the South, where his race might be an issue off the field. RJ hadn't heard of the subtle but pernicious contemporary racism that his mother spoke of, but she usually knew what she was talking about.

In the end, State seemed to be the best fit, based on his NFL goals and geography.

Chapter 7

THE FOLLOWING THURSDAY, Mya sent RJ a text saying that she couldn't make it to the game. Her car had broken down, and she had no way of driving the two hours to State. As he read the message for a second time, RJ felt depressed. *Damn, if I only had the cash to set her up with a new ride.*

Just last week, Kevin had suggested that Mya could get a new car from one of the agents if she wanted to.

"I don't want to be like that," RJ replied, knowing that it was true all the same.

"So your principles are going to cock-block you. That's your decision, man." Kevin left the room after that discussion. RJ found that Kevin spent more time outside of the room lately, and he wondered why.

He knew that he could likely get her to the game if he asked Coach, but RJ didn't want to go down that path.

He was still torn by what to do about his parents and grandfather, none of whom seemed to understand what they were doing, or how it could affect him. They'd taken their good fortune at face value, not looking under the façade to see what was really going on. His mother didn't question her good luck with her recent spate of assignments, and his grandfather knew that free rides to games for relatives was frowned upon.

RJ had dinner by himself that night, then went back to the room. He decided that he'd start on his English paper, even though it wasn't due until next Tuesday. It was better than moping around all evening, thinking about Mya and their lack of funds.

Kevin came in around 7 pm and looked at him. "Studying, dude? Really? It's Friday night. You need to loosen up and have some fun."

RJ shook his head slowly. "Nah, Mya can't come up this weekend, so my fun is postponed until her car is fixed."

Kevin shucked his shirt and threw it at him. "Man, she has you whipped. You can have fun without a woman, you know?"

RJ laughed at him. "When was the last time you had fun without a woman involved?"

Kevin laughed. "Dude, you asking me if I do men, or you asking if I can have fun without getting laid?"

RJ threw the shirt back at him. "You know what I mean. A whole night of hanging with your friends that doesn't involve a sock on the door when I get back."

"Yeah, I do that a lot. You might see that if you actually went out with us. We're not a terrible group of guys. We're just having some fun. You should try it."

RJ shrugged. "I don't drink much, so I—"

"See, there you go again. You haven't even gone out with us, and you're judging what we do and who we are. Not fair."

RJ considered Kevin's words. He was right, of course. RJ had never been out with the guys from the team. He'd made a lot of assumptions about them, based on what he'd experienced in high school. There, he'd pretty much ignored everything the team did. Since so many people wanted to be like him, he led by example. So he didn't drink, stayed faithful to his girl, and always tried to play his best game.

But now, even though he was proving himself, the culture at State was so well-entrenched that RJ doubted that he could ever change it by example. What did that leave him with, besides being lonely and doing his best?

"Okay, prove it to me," RJ said with a smile. "I'll go out tonight. No women and very little drinking, though. Right?"

Kevin grinned. "Absolutely. I can't believe that you're actually going. Some of the guys thought you'd go all four years, and never go out once with us."

RJ wondered what his reputation was, if this was the sort of speculation the others made about him. Maybe he needed to make a change.

Kevin hustled out, took a shower, and returned to the room. "You're still here. I wasn't sure if you'd decide to go to the library and study your brains out tonight."

Kevin threw on a pair of jeans and a polo shirt. He sprayed enough cologne on himself that the entire room smelled of spice and citrus. RJ knew that he'd reek of it, too.

RJ found a clean shirt and a nice pair of jeans to wear. He was looking for the right shoes, when Kevin pulled the LeBron's from under the bed. "If you're going out, go out in style. These are exactly what you need."

Kevin held the shoes out to him, and RJ waivered. The shoes had been sitting there for weeks. They technically weren't from a donor or agent, since they'd come from the school, albeit a grant provided by an alumnus. He finally took the shoes and slipped them on. Someone had already laced them. Had Kevin laced them, or had they come this way? RJ didn't remember, but was curious to know.

They were incredibly comfortable, and they did look good. RJ had to admit that these were some fine kicks, though a small part of his brain still worried about the rules involved in taking these shoes. However, this gift seemed mild, given what members of his own family were accepting.

He stood up and looked at them in the full-length mirror. They fit and suited him well. "Okay, I'm ready to go."

Kevin laughed. "Yes, you are."

They stopped on the first floor of the dorm, and two other guys joined them. RJ recognized Josh, who was one of the first-string fullbacks on the team. He gave RJ a nod, but didn't speak. The other guy was named Tony, but RJ didn't recognize him. He guessed that Tony had to be on another team at school. Tony spoke a few words to Kevin, but then they lapsed into silence as they walked uptown.

They stopped at a bar called McCabe's, and Kevin held the door open, making a welcoming motion to RJ. He wasn't sure how to take Kevin's gesture. Was he mocking him, or was he really happy that RJ was having a night out with them? RJ couldn't be sure at all.

The bartender seemed to know them, and slid three beers and a mixed drink at them. Kevin took the beers by the necks, and distributed them: one to RJ, one to Josh, and one for himself. Tony had a mixed drink that RJ couldn't identify.

RJ took a small swig of the beer, and tried not to make a face. He'd had beer before. His parents let him try different types of alcohol after he'd turned 16. They doled out small amounts to him over the years. He liked some of the mixed drinks, and sometimes a dark beer. But lagers and ales did nothing for him. To him, they tasted like urine.

They found a table where Josh and Tony took seats, so they could see everyone coming into the darkened bar. The four of them shot the shit for a while, until Tony spotted some girl that he'd hooked up with a few times. He promptly left the table. And Josh left a few minutes later to buy some blondes a drink at the bar.

Kevin looked at RJ and grinned. "So this isn't so bad, is it?"

RJ shook his head. "Not bad at all. I like the music."

Kevin laughed. "Yeah, that's what all the guys on the team come here for—the music."

RJ looked around. Both Josh and Tony were nowhere to be found. RJ assumed that both of them had already gotten lucky and left with someone.

"It's what I come here for, too. And the company." RJ gave him a smile.

"Yeah, I know. I'm a charmer. So what's up with you and this girlfriend? I'm guessing it's pretty serious if you're still exclusive here."

RJ told him all about Mya: How they'd met, how they'd been dating ever since, and what they hoped to do after graduation. Kevin actually seemed to be listening. His eyes were focused on RJ, and he wasn't scoping out every girl who came into the place. Maybe he'd been wrong about his roommate.

"I'm jealous. I'd love to know who my soulmate was so early in life. That would be a big worry off my mind." Kevin eyed RJ's beer, which was still pretty much untouched. He picked it up and drained it in a few gulps. "You don't drink, do you?"

"I drink. Just not a lager kind of guy. I like dark beer better."

Kevin nodded, left for the bar, and returned with two more beers. This time, one of them was dark. "Got you a Guinness. They don't come much darker than that."

RJ took a swig and smiled. It was much better. "So you're not dating anyone special, I'm guessing?"

Kevin snickered and took a long draw on his beer. "What was your first clue? The long stream of women in and out of the dorm room?"

"Yeah, that might have been a giveaway to me."

He shrugged. "I dated someone pretty special in high school. I even thought I was in love with her, but I caught her with my best friend. Actually walked in on them while they were doing it. I haven't bothered with relationships since then. They don't seem worth it."

RJ nodded. First loves are powerful. Maybe he was just being hard on Kevin, since he saw what his roommate did on a nightly basis.

"Yeah, sorry to hear that," RJ said. He took another swig of beer. He felt a little lightheaded. He knew that he was a lightweight, but he tried to keep it steady. No use showing Kevin that he couldn't hold his liquor.

Since Kevin had sucked down his beer, he walked off to the bar for another. When he returned, he had another dark beer for RJ as well. "You need to stop nursing those things and loosen up." He slid the beer across to RJ.

"So what were we talking about?" Kevin said after another drink from the bottle. "I think we've exhausted the topic of girls. How about football?"

RJ smiled. At least it hadn't turned into a grilling session. Since Kevin didn't want to know everything about him, RJ was glad for the surface talk.

Kevin told him about his rise to the college level, which sounded pretty much like RJ's own trajectory. He'd started in youth leagues and went on to win a few awards before going to State. He laughed about how much different college was than high school and youth leagues. "You think I'm just here to have fun, but I'm not. I know the pressure. I know the stakes. So sometimes I need to let loose and just have fun. If I couldn't do that, I'd go crazy."

"What about all the parties and the people and everything?"

"Man, don't ever trust all those people. Everyone here wants something for themselves. They don't care about what's best for you or what's best for your career. They want to make a dollar off of you. Don't forget that. My dad told me that, and it's the best advice he ever gave me. After my first year, I had people trying to sign me up for representation. Like a 19-year-old would know what's best for him in the NFL."

RJ thought about what Kevin was saying. He had to admit that he was a little jealous. He wished that his own dad would give him this kind of advice. He was in the sports industry, even though he was only a PE teacher. He could have used some advice from his dad. RJ was starting to see that his grandfather couldn't be trusted to manage every aspect of his career. While Grandpa had been a help growing up, he was out of touch at the college level, in terms of the plays that needed to be made and the decisions ahead.

RJ was surprised when he looked down to find that his second beer was gone. They'd been talking, and he had been absentmindedly drinking throughout the conversation. It didn't seem like he'd finished an entire bottle. This time, he got up—leaving a hand on the table to steady himself—and went to the bar to buy another round. He was surprised by the price, which took up most of his spending money for the week.

RJ took the two beers back to the table, and sat them down with care. He stood at the table for a minute, as he watched Kevin down a good portion of the new beer.

"Drink up, man. You need to blow off some steam." Kevin tilted his head back and finished the beer off. He smacked his lips as he finished, and put the beer back on the table.

RJ had never really drunk this much before. His parents' tastings were just that—small samples. And this was his third beer in less than an hour.

Kevin gave him a nudge, and RJ tilted the bottle up and felt the dark beer coat his throat on the way down. A few people shouted "chug" as he wrapped his lips around the bottle and made sure it all went down. He was feeling the buzz when he finished the bottle, and placed it down on the table. It clattered down onto the floor, and RJ laughed.

Kevin got them another round, and RJ found that this new round went down faster. He didn't remember much after that. He knew that some of the guys from the team showed up later. A few of them brought women over to talk to RJ, but he didn't really want to talk to them. He wanted to be a part of the team. And there were too many people at the table now to talk to anyone, especially with fans and occasional drunk women interrupting any conversation he was trying to finish. He tried to be polite about it, but he didn't want to flirt. Nevertheless, a few women paid for RJ's drinks, which he graciously accepted. He gradually lost count of how many drinks he'd had.

The next thing RJ knew, it was the next morning, and he was waking up in his own bed—with the sun in his eyes and a throbbing headache. Someone, presumably Kevin, had undressed him and put him in bed. But RJ didn't remember that at all.

Kevin was sitting at his desk, reading a book. "Here you are," he said, offering RJ a bottle of water and some pills. "Aspirin for your headache."

RJ downed the pills and finished the bottle of water. His mouth felt like the Sahara. "What time is it?" he asked, rubbing his eyes.

"A little after 11," Kevin replied without looking up.

"Shit, I missed my philosophy class." RJ had no idea what time he'd made it to bed, so he had no clue whether or not he'd gotten a good night's sleep.

"No worries. I had the RA call the prof and tell him that you were under the weather. All under control, bro."

RJ tried to wrap his head around that idea. He knew that his philosophy professor allowed two absences before it would affect his grade. It was only September, and he'd missed one class already. Taking classes while playing football would be tough enough, without being docked for attendance.

"Should I ask what happened?" RJ asked. Part of him wanted to fill in the missing time, while another part of him wasn't sure that he wanted to hear the answer.

"After the fourth beer, you were feeling it. We hung out. I got you a glass of water and made you drink it. Then I helped you home and put you to bed. Pretty standard wingman work."

"Thanks. Did the RA say anything about me being drunk?" RJ knew that State had tough standards about underage drinking, and he didn't want to jeopardize his scholarship over a good time.

Kevin laughed. "He said you were a fun drunk. Other than that, you're mild compared to what he normally has to deal with. He's cool unless there are kids under 18 or farm animals involved. That's his official motto."

RJ rolled over and hid his eyes from the sun. "Is this headache normal?"

"Pretty much. At first, it's bad, but then after you start getting used to them, you learn how to stop them before they start. I'm good after taking two aspirin and a liter of water before bed."

"Why didn't you give me those last night?"

"Dude, you were snoring by the time we got your head on the pillow. No way were you waking up for a liter of water." He laughed as he spoke.

RJ managed to take a shower and get ready for his afternoon classes. The headache subsided as he was able to squeeze in a bite to eat before the first class. When he finally checked his phone, he realized that he'd missed an 8 am call from Mya. He tried to think of what to tell her about last night, but nothing came to mind. She knew him well enough to know that he was inexperienced with drinking. He was sure that she'd have some less-than-kind words to say to him about this situation. Even so, she'd still be sympathetic about him being lonely and wanting to feel like a part of the group, especially since she hadn't been able to come up this weekend.

Practice that day was an absolute killer. Coach noticed that he was lethargic, and made a few comments about his performance. RJ assured him that he'd just had a hard week, and that he'd be fine by tomorrow.

"You sure this doesn't have anything to do with last night?" Coach pointedly asked.

RJ started, embarrassed that the man knew about his attempt at partying. "Maybe a little. I went overboard last night. I'm not a drinker." RJ wondered who'd ratted him out. Since he couldn't even remember who'd been at the bar last night, he wasn't sure who it might have been.

"Look, RJ, I'm here to help. I'm not going to tell you to never drink, because that's unreasonable. But I will remind you that you wouldn't try to keep time with a miler when you run. So don't try to keep up with Kevin when he drinks. He makes it look easy—like there are no consequences. But that's not true. He'd probably be in the NFL by now if he'd stop drinking and focus on the game. I don't want to see you go down the same path."

RJ just nodded. He knew that Coach was right. He just wanted to fit in and have friends for an evening. Now he was paying for it, because the opinions that really mattered were being damaged. He sighed and headed to the locker room.

The atmosphere was different today. A few guys were left in the changing area, who joked with RJ about getting drunk and told him he needed to drink a shower's worth of water to ditch a hangover. They weren't the sort of interactions he wanted, but he was just glad for the conversation. He laughed with them, dressed, and made his way back to the dorm.

He caught dinner and headed back to the room to study. He called Mya first, knowing that she was going to be mad.

RJ was surprised to find out that she wasn't upset with him because she was feeling frustrated about being one of the only girls in a tech program. Most of her classes were comprised of boys, and many of them acted like they'd never seen a girl up close before. She was treated awkwardly and differently, and she didn't like it. RJ liked listening to her complain about the conversations at her school, which dealt more with superheroes than technology.

That's what he loved about Mya. She took him as he was. She understood him and loved him without question. She could talk to him about anything, and he knew that she'd listen to him. Even though he'd been scared that he'd let her down, she made him feel better by sharing a part of herself. Damn, he was lucky.

RJ went to bed at 9 pm that night, knowing that the bus for the away game left at 8 the next morning. Kevin wasn't home at 2 am when RJ had to hit the bathroom to get rid of the water that everyone had given him that day. Coach was right. Kevin managed to get drunk and still function on the field, but few were that lucky.

The game on Saturday was televised, so he knew that his family would be watching. He knew that Mya would be watching somewhere too. He'd skipped the call to his grandfather, knowing that the older man would not likely be up by the time that he had to leave the dorm. RJ would call later and explain what had happened.

There was no "play" in this game against Langley State. Sportscasters predicted an LS win against State, except a few who suggested that RJ would be a factor in the game. RJ tried not to take the comments personally. He didn't want his head to get too big, and he didn't want to put too much pressure on himself, due to the comments of a few men who were too old to play the game.

Instead of a play, RJ just kept hitting passes time after time. In fact, he set a new school record for State of total passing yards in one game. RJ did note that the one time he'd tried to pass to Kevin, the ball slipped through his fingers, and had been called an incomplete. Kevin tried to blame it on an interference from the LS team, but RJ hadn't seen it. And judging from Coach's face, he hadn't either.

Maybe the drinking was actually catching up with Kevin. But RJ didn't have time to think about that now. He was only interested in winning the game. By the end of the game, RJ set a new record, and State won 28-17. The bus ride home was loud and boisterous.

RJ managed to get in touch with his grandfather when he got home. He explained the early departure, and how it had affected his schedule.

"No problem at all, kid. No problem. I figured it was something like that. Don't worry about me. We've got enough games under our belts that one missed game won't change us." Grandpa laughed and started telling RJ about the plaque that State was planning to put in the stadium—to mark this new record. "I'll be down for that ceremony. You can count on it."

RJ wondered how his grandfather had heard about the record already. Had an agent told him, or had the news already reported it?

RJ hung up the phone, feeling slightly disconnected from the people he should feel closest to. He missed Mya, who'd told him that it could be two weeks before her car was fixed. Now he'd skipped calling his grandfather before a game. It was as if he was breaking away from his past, and he didn't like that feeling at all.

He was surprised that his parents hadn't called him. His mom usually called to talk about the game, even if his dad seldom did. But tonight, his phone was silent. He missed them, too, and wished that they'd called about the win. State was off to a great start, and many of the commentators credited RJ with that record.

Chapter 8

AS THE NEXT week rolled around, RJ was shocked to learn about the midterm expectations for all his classes. The weekly work suddenly tripled, with papers and projects due in every class. But since Coach wasn't slowing down their practice schedule, RJ found himself with no free time at all. He went from the field to the library, and made it back to the room at 3 or 4 in the morning to start it all again.

By Wednesday, he was exhausted. Coach called him out on the field twice for screwing up an easy play. It felt like he had to run suicides and drills after practice because he studied, rather than slept and partied. RJ felt a surge of anger at Coach, the team, and the expectations of the school—that it was easier to coast through college than it was to actually get an education.

He went back to the room, took a shower, and tried to determine what he'd work on that night. He had papers due in English and philosophy. He just thought he'd start on the first, and work until he fell asleep.

Kevin was in the room when he returned, and he smiled at him as he came in. "Want to try another night out? Looks like you could use one."

"I could," RJ lied. He didn't like the lethargic feeling he had when he was hungover. He needed a pick-me-up, and told Kevin as much.

"I got just the thing for you, man. Hold on. I'll be right back." Kevin left the room without another word, and was gone for several minutes. When he returned, he had a small plastic bag full of something.

"Take a sniff of this."

"Man, I'm not doing cocaine. What are you, crazy?"

Kevin laughed, a loud guffaw that shocked RJ. "I don't walk around with bagfuls of illegal drugs, dude. This here is Ritalin. Just what the doctor ordered."

"What is it?" RJ eyed the bag and its contents. He'd heard of the drug, but he wasn't familiar with the specifics.

"It's a prescription drug that's used to calm down hyper kids and make them focus more."

"I don't need to calm down. I need to be that hyper kid." RJ checked the clock and noticed the time. He was spending way too much time on this conversation. He needed to be talking less and writing more. He had work to do.

Kevin laughed again. "It has the opposite effect on us. It makes us hyper. We can still focus, but it keeps us awake. It's just what you need for these papers. I hope you've learned a lesson—not to try to do too much during football season."

RJ nodded. "I thought this wasn't too much for the season. I thought I was taking it easy."

"Yeah, everyone always thinks that football players take easy classes, because they're too dumb to take anything harder," Kevin said. "It's not like that. If you have an away game on Saturday, you miss Friday classes. Same for a Sunday game and missing Monday. Plus practices and other events. Add all that up, and you barely have time to attend classes, much less do the work. Then if you don't keep your grade-point up, you're out of the school for good. So the easier, the better."

RJ nodded. "I'm starting to see that. I thought I'd be different. I wanted to get a good education."

Kevin held out the bag. "Don't we all? I was going to be a mechanical engineer, but I can't even attend all the classes. And the fieldwork is impossible to get completed with my schedule. So it's undeclared for me."

RJ looked at the time again. He'd lost nearly an hour on the shower and the conversation. He was screwed tonight, because he'd only have one or two hours before he'd fall asleep. He could already feel his eyes start drooping. There was no way he'd finish the papers in time for his classes that week.

"So I hate to be ignorant, but how do I take this stuff? With a glass of water, or do I just swallow them?"

Kevin held a finger to his nose and inhaled sharply. "Sniff it."

Kevin poured a handful into his palm and held it out for RJ. He leaned into the other man's palm and inhaled sharply. The drug went up into his nose, and the first reaction he had was that the inside of his nose was on fire. Maybe that was how it kept you awake. Pain always prevents sleep. After thirty seconds or so, the pain started to subside.

Within a few minutes, RJ began feeling a buzz in his brain. He was anxious to get started on his papers. He looked at Kevin and said, "Thanks. You won't tell anyone about this, right?"

Kevin grinned and crossed his heart with a finger. "Not me. I'm not a snitch. Besides, as my roomie, think of what you could say about me."

RJ nodded. "I just need to be sure. I'm going to the library now. See you sometime."

Kevin smiled and waved.

RJ stayed up until 4 am that night. He finished both papers and studied for his history midterm. He knew that 9 am would roll around quickly, so he forced himself to go to bed before the sun came up.

RJ found that he didn't grow tired over the course of the day, and Coach actually complimented him on his performance at practice later that day. Of course, by the time he came home and had dinner, the effects of the drug had worn off. Then he felt slow and sleepy, in the face of two midterm exams the following day.

Kevin wasn't around that evening. RJ hesitated about going through Kevin's personal belongings, but he wanted that feeling back of being invincible and having unlimited strength. It wasn't something he normally felt, even though he was strong and in the prime of his youth.

RJ's search didn't turn up anything. He had to call another player on the team, and admit that he didn't have his own roommate's phone number. The guy laughed about it, but gave him the digits without protesting.

Kevin picked up on the third ring, which gave RJ enough time to get nervous. He'd fail both tests if he couldn't study that night. No matter how well he did on the field, he'd be kicked out of school before the scouts could see him in action—if he couldn't keep his grades up. He knew he'd be fine if he could be discovered. But until then, he had to be on his best behavior.

"That you, roomie? What's up? Is it party time?" Kevin laughed. RJ could hear girls' voices in the background. "How are those papers? You all done?"

RJ explained his need for more of the Ritalin for his midterm exams the following day. "You have to help me."

Kevin laughed again. "Oh man, you don't know what you're asking. I'm here with three girls. Count them: three. And only two of them are undressed now. And I have to leave so you can get an A on a test? Shit."

RJ felt his chest constrict. He didn't know what he'd do if Kevin said no. He could already feel his eyelids growing heavy. He needed a bump to get by.

"Look, give me an hour, and I'll be home, okay? And I'll have your stuff." Kevin hung up before RJ could respond. He guessed it would have to be okay. He didn't have any other choice at that moment.

An hour later, when Kevin came home, RJ was sound asleep in bed. He'd woken to Kevin shaking his arm, and calling his name. "Dude, you have it bad. Wake up. I'm here with your magic wake-up pills."

RJ sat up, embarrassed that he had so little strength to resist sleep for an hour. He knew that he needed the pills right then. It was more than just a want: They were necessary for him to get by. He panicked for a minute, thinking that he was becoming reliant on a drug. But he reminded himself that it was a prescription medication, so it couldn't be all that bad.

Kevin held out a hand like before, and RJ sniffed loudly as the drug went up his nose. He waited for the rush of the pills to come over him. And again, within minutes, he was wide awake and focused. RJ gave Kevin a quick one-armed hug, grabbed an armful of books, and headed to the library to study.

RJ didn't even bother with sleep that night. He stayed up until 5 am, then opted to stay awake until his first class started. He felt good about the results of each of the tests, though he wouldn't know how he'd done for another week.

But he was sluggish again at practice that day. But this time, there were no extra sprints. He was called into the coach's office after practice. He was nervous, and the adrenaline of the situation made him feel wide awake again.

"What's up, Coach?"

"RJ, is something going on?"

"No sir."

"Well, I've been keeping an eye on you this week, and you haven't been the player I've seen all season. You're sluggish and tired—out of focus. We've got a big game this weekend, and I can't have you falling asleep on the field."

"With midterms and all, it's just been a hard week. I've just been overwhelmed by the amount of work I've had to do. I had to pull an all-nighter to study for two tests last night. It's been a tough week."

Coach sighed, and looked at him, as if he knew something else was happening. RJ panicked, wondering if Kevin had shared what he'd done for him. "Are you sure there's nothing else? You'd tell me, right?"

RJ nodded. "Nothing at all. I promise, I'll be fine tomorrow. I'm going to go home and catch up on my sleep. I'll be ready for tomorrow. I promise."

The coach looked at him for a long minute, while RJ fidgeted like a kindergartener who'd been caught eating extra cookies. "Fine, but if you're doing anything that's affecting your performance, I'll have no problem yanking you from the game. You know that, right? I only want players who give this game their all. Nothing less."

RJ nodded and gulped hard. He felt like the coach had seen through his lies, and had learned the truth about what was going on. He felt as exposed as if he was standing there naked. The coach seemed to know what was going on with his players.

RJ returned to his dorm room in silence. None of the other players had waited around for him. He figured that most of them were deciding which parties they would attend later, or figuring out who they'd be going out with that night. RJ would be eating dinner and going to bed early, as if he was being punished by his parents. He didn't used to mind. He'd gotten into the routine of doing it long ago, but somehow, it was harder now.

He'd hung out with some of the other players. He'd spent two evenings at the library, and had actually had the time to feel like a real college student. He'd seen others studying, and knew that they felt the same pressures to succeed in school. He'd missed the camaraderie of the students so far that year. Most of the time, he'd spent his study time in the room, hoping that Kevin would find another place to carouse.

But he and Kevin finally seemed to be connecting after months of being strangers in a confined space. He liked their new relationship better. And he could still remember the rush of those pills, and he thought about asking Kevin for more. But RJ knew that those pills were nothing but trouble for him. He'd seen too many others get dependent on pills and other drugs.

In high school, one of his biggest rivals in the county was a kid who'd gone from 210 to 240 pounds in just three months. The guy was defined and ripped. RJ suspected steroids, but of course, he could hardly accuse him of abuse, since he barely knew him. It wasn't until the city tournament that things came to a head. The player ended up striking his coach so hard that he had to go to the hospital. He was suspended with the threat of expulsion, and the team spectacularly lost during the first round of the tournament.

So RJ knew that drugs could destroy people. He kept that in mind as he nearly fell asleep while he was eating alone in the dining hall. His head hit the pillow at 8 pm, and he woke the following morning feeling refreshed and not needing medication.

He'd missed a few calls from family and Mya while he'd been asleep. His mom had left a message saying that her workload for this new client had doubled, which meant that they wouldn't be coming to the game. She offered no excuse for why his father wouldn't be there. He'd never come to many of RJ's games, typically only when she forced him to. RJ shrugged, now knowing their pattern all too well. He didn't expect it to change now.

His grandfather had called as well, saying that he hoped they could talk about the game on Friday night. Apparently, he was going somewhere on Saturday afternoon, and RJ was immediately suspicious that the situation involved Edward Donley. He hoped that his grandfather wasn't getting too connected to the alumnus with deep pockets. His coach had discouraged the weekly talks. But perhaps now his grandfather was being given these perks to keep him too busy to offer RJ advice. Bribery would serve both causes well.

Mya called to tell him that she'd gotten a job interview at an IT firm. To help her pay for college, she'd be working part-time. So instead of working two jobs to make ends meet, she'd just have one better-paying job that allowed her time to visit RJ at school. Again, he was instantly wary about the timing of the interview. He logged onto the computer and looked for any connection between Donley and the company Mya had mentioned. But he found nothing. He was sweating by the time he finished his search. RJ wondered: *Was he being paranoid about this, or were these perks just coming too quickly and frequently to be a coincidence?*

He only opted to call Mya back. She was the only one of the three that wouldn't leave him with doubts about her loyalty to him. But they'd all seemed to easily take things that were offered to them, without either thinking or caring.

RJ didn't want his own life to go that way. He wanted a life that was discussed and considered. Even his mother had jumped at a job, thinking that it had been offered because of her skills, rather than being an incentive. They were all enjoying the largesse of life—the things that he couldn't enjoy yet. It seemed so unfair.

RJ had read about World War II, when people saved and rationed for four years. Then the boom of spending occurred after the war was over. Having no reason to pinch pennies anymore, the country went mad about buying things. Now he thought of his own life, and wondered if he would be the same. If he even got a six-figure contract, would he spend everything that came his way? Would he demand a big house and flashy cars during his first year?

He really didn't know. He was only three months into his freshman year. And he was already complaining about the huge money he generated for the school, while earning nothing in return.

Mya wasn't answering, so RJ decided to go to breakfast. Nothing heavy, but he needed something for his body after the rollercoaster ride of the past few days. He needed to get back to normal and be more even-keeled. He finished his breakfast alone, returned to the dorm, got his gear ready for the game, and headed out to find the bus.

The team they were playing against had lost every game so far. So RJ wasn't worried about this game, except for Coach's threats to possibly bench him. RJ didn't want the speculation that he'd done something wrong on the air. He wasn't used to media attention, but he knew that his absence would be noticed and discussed, since he'd started every game this year. The mere thought of that struck him with panic.

As it turned out, RJ was benched for part of the game for different reasons: The score at the end of the first half was 34-0. Coach put the second-string quarterback into the game, along with most of the second-string defenders. Their only goal was to maintain, which they did. RJ sat out the rest of the game, watching from the sidelines and deciding that this place didn't suit him well. He much preferred being in the game, where his presence brought the team attention and media discussions.

The ride on the bus back to campus was subdued. They'd won, but it was not a hard-fought, particularly difficult win. The game had almost been handed to them. RJ was slightly annoyed to hear that several scouts for the NFL had been at the game. He'd played well for the first half, but he'd sat out for two quarters, which gave the scouts no time to see him in action. While he wished the backup quarterback all the best, he didn't want it to come at his own expense.

The following week was an away game, but it required a flight out on Thursday night—with a return on Monday morning. The game was in the Midwest, and RJ knew that it would gain more national attention than some of the recent games. He was excited about the chance to show off for a new audience.

So he was understandably shocked when his philosophy professor assigned a ten-page paper that was due on Tuesday morning. He tried to talk to the professor after class, explaining that he would be out of town for the next three days. However, RJ just received the old meme that, as a student athlete, "student" came before "athlete." He could understand that sentiment in high school, but in college, the football revenue paid this man's salary. He could pontificate the role of education all he wanted, but the truth was that he relied on guys like RJ to make a living.

RJ walked back to the dorm in silence. He didn't know what to do. The paper was worth enough of his grade for the semester that failing would tank his grades and his scholarship. But he would have no time to write and proof a ten-pager. He had to produce it, but he had no way of making that happen.

For a moment, he thought about asking Mya to do it. But given the topic, she would have to spend twice as much time researching it as writing it. The end product wouldn't illustrate that he'd been in class all term.

He was lying on his bed and staring at the ceiling when Kevin came in. He explained the situation to his roommate, who again used the occasion to complain about the expectations for athletes at a major university. And that didn't help RJ one bit.

Kevin hadn't been able to provide a solution. He'd called his grandfather later that evening, so he could explain the situation and ask for advice. The older man agreed that RJ was caught between a rock and a hard place. There wasn't a solution.

At ten that evening, there was a knock on the door. A courier stood there with a manila envelope with RJ's name on it. The man handed him the envelope and left without a word. RJ wondered what it could be. He'd never seen a courier before, and he was curious about who could be sending him something this way.

RJ swallowed hard when he opened the envelope. It was a ten-page paper for his philosophy class and a flash drive. He flipped through it. The paper didn't have an author's name or any other identifying marks on it. The paper was white, clean, and fresh. It looked as if it had just been printed out.

Sitting down at his computer, RJ opened the flash drive, which only held one file. He opened the file and copied a section of the paper into the plagiarism website that all the TAs used. It passed without question. The work was original and unmarked.

RJ knew that he had to read it. His decisions would be made for him if the paper contained incorrect information or was poorly written. But as he read the pages, the style and clarity of the prose made RJ slightly jealous. It was definitely something he could have written, but hadn't. There was nothing in the text that was far above his current level, which made it entirely believable that the paper was his own.

Where had it come from? RJ had to know. He'd only shared his concerns about his class with a few people. The most likely suspects were his grandfather and Kevin.

RJ had already seen his grandfather in action—taking rides in fancy cars and going on trips that were presumably all-expenses-paid. His grandfather had always been his biggest supporter, so it was likely that he'd stretch things to produce a paper that would keep RJ in school.

However, Kevin was equally likely. He somehow had access to a lot of money. There was no way that selling the gym shoes had lasted this long. He'd seen firsthand how Kevin spent at the bar, which would take hundreds of dollars on a weekly basis. And Kevin had never said where he'd gotten the Ritalin from, but it had been almost immediately available to him. Kevin seemed to be the go-to man for finding anything RJ needed. A concierge for the athlete of today.

In any case, the paper was perfect, and RJ had a decision to make. He knew that neither his grandfather nor Kevin would tell the professor or Coach about it. However, if someone like Edward Donley provided the cash to produce that paper, then he'd have a pipeline to RJ.

RJ rationalized that he already had one. His mother worked for Osmond Publishing, and they could cut her in a second, since she was a freelancer. RJ knew that his mother loved that work, but it was unstable and uncertain. However, she'd lost major clients before and survived. Presumably, she could do it again.

His grandfather's perks were less tangible. A ride and some travel. Nothing overt, nothing that could be taken away and cause injury. His grandfather was always sly in that regard. He knew people, and he understood how the world worked.

However, this paper was a different matter. RJ had to call it cheating—because that's what it was. He was passing off someone else's work for his own. That could cause him to be expelled from school. No school, no scholarship, no team, no NFL.

However, RJ had to be honest. He had no other way to complete a paper and turn it in. His only computer was the desktop in his room. He couldn't afford a laptop or a tablet. It was all his parents could afford, and even that had taken some scrimping to manage. He had to be at his desk to write. No way around it.

RJ took a deep breath. He clicked on the paper, added his name and course number to the title page, and printed it out.

Just then, Kevin came in and began throwing some things into a bag. "Man, I can't wait to get out of here. I need a break, you know?"

RJ nodded, thinking of school and Mya, and knowing that the last thing he needed was time away. He missed his girl, and he needed more time for school. Away games were the worst for both of his needs.

RJ threw the paper on his desk and began to pack as well.

The game went well. State was the easy winner over Midwestern U, despite the predictions of many of the talking heads. RJ passed for nearly 250 yards, which was a solid game. And the defense was fantastic. Their opponents didn't stand a chance. The team returned home to a crowd of fans and media. It took RJ nearly 45 minutes to get from the airport back to the dorm, which was usually only a 15-minute drive.

When he got back to his dorm room, the paper was still on his desk, but the headiness from the weekend was blurring the moral lines for him a little. He was skilled at playing football. He was meant to play football. Perhaps others around him were just starting to see that. He took the paper as being his due as an elite player. Why shouldn't he? Others around here accepted much larger gifts than a ten-page paper.

He turned in the paper, and watched as the professor collected the papers from the rest of the class and stacked them on his desk. It was done now. There was no turning back.

Over the next few days, when RJ thought about the paper, his chest grew tight. Yet nothing happened. The grades were posted on Thursday, and RJ got a B+. Not perfect, but nothing that would set off the alarm bells that he'd cheated. The matter seemed settled, and RJ wanted to put it behind him.

He had bigger things on his mind anyway. After he returned, two agents were practically parked in the lobby of the dorm, waiting for him. They quickly explained that they both wanted to represent him. They talked to him about endorsement deals in the future, and his potential in the NFL.

RJ put them both off, but the feeling that his dreams were so close was beyond anything he could describe. RJ could taste the acclaim and the money. It was the culmination of everything he and his grandfather had worked for since the age of nine. Why shouldn't he enjoy the fruits of his labors?

It took every ounce of willpower to walk past them and up to his room.

But RJ also knew that ineligibility only really started when the value of the gifts exceeded $100,000. For most of the small stuff, the money merely had to be repaid. He knew that his family didn't have much, so that might be an issue. But it wouldn't derail RJ's plans for the NFL. Everything could be paid off after he went to the big game.

Both of them were still sitting there when he returned to the lobby to head to dinner. They were persistent, if nothing else. They both followed him this time, walking with him as he headed to the dining hall.

The first agent was tall, thin, and dark-haired, and looked at the dining hall in disgust. "We can go somewhere better if you'd like. We don't have to eat here."

The second agent was blonde and looked like a former linebacker. But he was red-faced, as though the pace was a bit much for him now. RJ walked a bit faster, hoping to tire the man out. "Anywhere you'd like. Steak, seafood. You name it."

"I'm fine here. I eat at the dining hall almost every night," RJ said, pasting a smile on his face. He'd met too many of these men through his grandfather. They wanted to make a quick buck on the backs of someone else. They were quick with their words, but most of them looked like they had lived the high life for far too long.

The two men stopped at the door. RJ was glad that they didn't come inside. He'd brought his history textbook to do that week's reading. He paused for a few minutes, wondering if either of them had played a role in delivering the research paper. If so, would they be offended by his desire to eat in the dining hall? He made a mental note to be polite to the men, though firm in not wanting to sign with an agent in the near future.

Both men were waiting for him as he left the dining hall. RJ wondered if they would be following him around all day. It was slightly unnerving to have these men buzz around him like flies.

The dark-haired man handed him a leather-bound folder. "Just look at this when you have a moment. It details some of my clients, and some of the endorsement deals I've gotten for them. I think you'll be impressed. Call me after you've watched it. You don't want to go pro without someone in place to guide you."

"Who said anything about going pro in the near future? I have three and a half years of school left." RJ was puzzled. The man seemed to act like the NFL was imminent.

"I heard it on CBS Sports last weekend. There are speculations that you'll start looking after your bowl game." The man spoke like he'd just found a $100 bill on the street. His grin was predatory, not friendly.

"I heard it on Fox," the other man joined in. "They were picking likely bowl games, and at the rate things were going, they said that you would likely go pro after this year."

RJ frowned. "What bowl game did they pick us for?"

"Rose or Cotton," the former linebacker replied. "That's not the important thing. You just need to go to any bowl game and do well. After that, you'll be set to be a first- or second-round draft selection."

The linebacker held out a flash drive on a keychain. "Here's my portfolio. Play your cards right, and there could be something else on the keychain. You know what

I'm saying, right?" He gave RJ a wink that appeared conspiratorial.

RJ just nodded at the men, and went back into his dorm. He didn't get rid of the portfolios as he'd originally planned, as the fine leather and nice keychain made him feel less inclined to dump them in the trash. They seemed too upscale for the garbage can.

After he sat down on his bed, he opened up the leather-bound portfolio. He was surprised to see two familiar NFL quarterbacks on the cover page. He began reading about how this agent—who was apparently named Max Armstrong—had helped shepherd these players through the draft process. There had been discussions with several of the team owners about the prospective draft. Of course, Max had peppered several photos of him schmoozing with team owners throughout the portfolio. He was definitely well-connected.

However, Armstrong clearly did not play fair. On the final pages of the portfolio, he had photos of the cars and homes of those quarterbacks. RJ was immediately envious. He wanted that lifestyle, and now it was so close to being within reach. He just had to keep doing what he'd been doing for a while longer.

Next, he walked over to his desk and plugged the flash drive into his computer. Images and text instantly filled his screen. The sound level surprised him, so he immediately turned down the volume. He started reading, and learned that "the linebacker" was named Fred Mertens. RJ recalled the name, and realized that he hadn't seen him play for several years. Would that happen to him? One day, he'd fade into retirement, and young players would have trouble remembering who he was? The thought depressed him. He wanted to be a legend in the game—to make an impact. Did these men just offer cash and a lifestyle, or did they really help cement a player's position in the history of the game?

While RJ was pondering this situation, Kevin and a couple of other guys he didn't recognize came in. Kevin ripped off his shirt and went to the closet to get a new one. RJ assumed that Kevin would be going out and taking his posse with him, since Sunday was technically a weeknight. He wondered if Kevin ever spent any time alone.

"What's this?" one of the other guys asked. "Is it a game or something?"

RJ looked at the guy. "No, it's an agent's portfolio. I had two guys trying to get me to sign with them today."

Kevin spun around. "Oh man, tell me you said yes. Just tell me you said yes."

RJ turned back to the screen. "Sure, I just signed with the first person that came along. I don't care whether or not they're good for my career. They were just the first."

Kevin stared at RJ so hard that he felt compelled to fully turn toward him. "What?"

Kevin swallowed hard. "I've been here for three years, and no one has offered to represent me. You're here three months, and you've got two jokers wanting to sign you. And you sound pissed. I don't get you, Robinson. I don't get you at all."

The other guys mumbled their assent.

"Man, it's just like anything else. You don't just take the first because it's the first. You take the best."

Kevin gave him a grin. "I think I'll tell your girlfriend that. Didn't you tell me that she was your first?"

RJ didn't like those implications. In fact, he didn't like Kevin even talking about Mya. Kevin's love life was everything that his relationship with Mya wasn't: shallow, indiscriminate, and even nasty at times.

"That's a little different. We have tons in common." RJ tried to focus on the screen and tune out his roommate's words.

"Yeah, yeah," Kevin joked. "I'm just taking your advice, and applying it to women. I'm looking for the best." The other guys laughed at that. RJ didn't like how easily they followed along with him. They needed a better role model.

RJ flipped through the webpages on the flash drive, which featured photos of homes, cars, and a lifestyle that RJ had dreamed of.

"Hey, are those agents still here? Maybe they can spot us some drinks tonight." Kevin rummaged for some cologne on his shelves.

"I don't know. They gave me the portfolios, and I came back here to look at them and have a quiet evening." RJ hoped that Kevin would get the hint.

"That's too bad. I've heard that they'll buy for the whole bar, just to get around the NCAA rules. Free always tastes better to me."

Kevin and the two guys stopped at the door. "You want to come with us? You can point them out if you see them."

RJ looked at another page of marketing hype on his computer, and turned it off. There was no use in daydreaming about the future right now. If he just maintained things the way they were, it would be here soon enough.

He looked around the room. He'd finished his work for the evening. The papers and readings had subsided since midterms, so he had an easy week in front of him. "Sure, I'll go out for a while."

RJ grabbed his phone and wallet. He wasn't interested in the same things as these guys, so he wasn't going to dress up. No reason to bother.

The agents had apparently left. They weren't in the lobby, which RJ was grateful for. In a way, he felt that he was leading them on by not making any commitments—a football tease, as it were. He tried to tell himself that they encountered this situation all the time, but it still niggled in the back of his brain. Should he even interact with them this season?

These words kept coming back to him: Go pro at the end of this season. The mere thought of being a pro thrilled him.

Kevin wanted to go to the same bar, McCabe's. When they got there, it wasn't crowded. RJ really hadn't expected a big crowd on a Sunday night, but it was still good to get out of the room.

When RJ ordered a water, Kevin groaned. "You should be celebrating, but instead, you're drinking water. What's the matter with you?"

RJ opened his wallet and showed the empty pouch to the other guys. "No cash, no drink." It really sucked to be so close to millions, and yet so far. He'd been studying myths in English, and he thought of some of the characters who'd suffered through a similar situation:

The man who was just out of reach of food, and starved as a result.

The guy who had to carry a rock up a hill, only to have it roll back down.

It was just like every new league and every new school: Start over, and see if you can prove yourself. Those stories never ended well, but RJ truly hoped that his story would end better.

Kevin shooed away RJ's wallet and ordered a round of shots—something called Jaegerbombs. When the drinks arrived, he felt the pressure to do the shot, along with the rest of them.

After the shot, RJ was inspired to reroute the conversation. "So one of the agents today was telling me that State's likely to go to a bowl game. Have you guys heard that?"

One of Kevin's friends was a blonde guy who looked too slender to play college football. He answered. "Yeah, my dad was telling me that the Rose Bowl was mentioned. How cool would that be? We'd all be on TV, and all those models. Damn, I might be too tired to play." He laughed at his own joke. "We only got four more games this season. We're 5-1 at the moment, and the games we have lined up aren't too bad. We could easily be 9-1."

Kevin shook his head. "That won't get us into the Rose Bowl. Our schedule is too weak. I'm thinking Cotton or maybe Sugar. You can tell I'm old-school. I don't call them by all those corporate names. It only reminds me that other people are making even more money off us than before."

RJ nodded. He liked all of the old bowl names as well, before corporations had taken over. Who wanted a Go Daddy Bowl? How many fans were going to host a website because of a football game?

"That's cool," RJ said. "I hadn't even thought that far ahead yet. I'm just focusing on the next game, you know?"

Kevin laughed. "I've been at this for three years, and I always look at the long haul. What's on the horizon for me? That's what I need to know. Next year will be my draft year, so I want to have the best year possible."

RJ nodded. It wasn't his philosophy, but he understood it. His grandfather had often told him to only focus on the next game, because worrying about the long-term future only led to worries.

"So you definitely think it's a possibility, though? I hadn't even thought about bowl games until they mentioned them."

Kevin ordered another round of shots. "Hell yeah. The media has a boner for you. Your little play from earlier this season has put you on the map. They'll want you in a bowl game for sure, because they want the ratings. Simple as that."

RJ nodded. He was less sure of how to ask the next question without sounding arrogant. "The agents also said something about this being my last year here. Have you heard that too, or are they blowing smoke up my ass?" He used a curse word, in an attempt to fit in. He hoped that making it sound like a question would be enough to not piss them off. RJ still wanted to fit in, even though the chances were that he'd be the only one at the table to ever get drafted. It sounded conceited, but it was the truth.

The fourth guy laughed and downed his third shot. "We've all heard the rumors. A couple of the players asked Coach, but his answer was about the same as yours: Keep your eye on the next game, not what might happen in the future."

RJ nodded. That sounded like something Coach would say, but it danced around the question itself: Were these agents telling the truth?

Kevin shoved another shot in his direction. RJ sucked it down in a gulp, and put the glass back on the table. He was cutting himself off at three drinks that night. He didn't want a repeat of last time. He'd felt like shit the next day, and it had helped push him into the mess with the philosophy paper. He didn't want to get behind again like he had with midterms.

Kevin left shortly after that round, and the other two players also didn't have any money. So they just sat and talked for a while. Both of them shared Kevin's viewpoint: Don't complain about the fact that agents are looking to sign you.

RJ listened to what they had to say. It was great to be talking to other guys on the team besides Kevin. His grandfather was still away, and wouldn't be back until the next day. His father preferred not to talk about football at all. He'd rather talk about school or books he'd read. Of course, his mother loved him and rooted for him, but she didn't understand what was involved with signing with an agent. RJ planned to talk to Coach the next day and see what he thought, but he probably wouldn't want to indulge in the speculation that RJ could be playing for the NFL the next year.

Three girls came to the table, and it seemed like they'd already decided who was getting whom, because they sat down in such a way that each girl faced one boy. The girl who'd selected RJ was blonde and blue-eyed, and had large breasts that she rubbed on his arms twice before he got up and left. Even with the drinks, he wouldn't cheat on Mya, just because the others were hooking up. He was better than that.

Chapter 9

RJ's MEETING WITH Coach went about as well as expected. Coach had listened patiently to what the agents had said. He was silent for a long time, so long that RJ wondered if he was going to reply at all.

"Son, don't listen to what everyone has to say about your life. You need to do what's best for you at the moment—not for the NFL, not for the pro coaches, and certainly not for the agents. I asked you to come here because you have a good head on your shoulders. And I don't want to see a bunch of hangers-on mess with that. Okay?"

RJ nodded, but his mind was still reeling from the possibilities.

He spent the better part of the day trying to think about other things. He had an easy week of classes and a home game on Saturday. He could still stay busy and keep his mind occupied. That way, he wouldn't overanalyze what he'd been told.

The week flew by without a problem. Mya texted twice to say that she'd be able to make it to the game. She'd been saving her money from the new job, and since she was only working one job, she had enough time to attend. He knew better than to ask his parents to attend. Mom would come if asked, but Dad would have some lame reason about why he couldn't be bothered. RJ tried to call his grandfather twice, but there was no answer. Even after he left messages, Grandpa didn't call him back.

Game day was bright and crisp: A beautiful day at the beginning of November. RJ was thrilled to see Mya before the game. He hadn't seen her in weeks, and he gave her a long hug, with the promise of more later. She gave him a big smile and held him tight. Mya was full of stories about school. Apparently, most of the boys there listened to her stories about RJ, even if they had no interest in sports or football. They just liked being around her. RJ worried for a moment. He wondered if she'd been away too long. Instead of complaining about them, it sounded like she liked them now. However, the panic subsided as she gave him another kiss.

He pointed to where her seat was, and he went to get dressed for the game. Amidst the cheers and shouts of the home crowd, he came out onto the field. He looked up to where Mya was supposed to be sitting, but there were so many people that he couldn't pick her out. He was just glad she was there. He remembered all the high school games she'd sat through, and how it had given him confidence to know she was there for him.

The first quarter was pretty lame. The defense was weak for some reason, and they scored twice against State. RJ was able to even the score up by the half, but it wasn't one of their best performances. RJ wished that Mya had been there for an earlier game, where she could have seen him shine. But he gave himself a talking to, reminding himself that she'd seen him shine in any number of previous games.

The third quarter started with State in possession of the ball. RJ called a play, and the team went into formation. He caught the ball and went to hand it off to a receiver, but there was no one there. RJ looked around in a panic, wondering where the player had gone. He couldn't even find him on the field. However, he could see two mountains of men barreling toward him at a faster speed than he liked.

Then RJ discovered that Kevin—of all people—was at their 20-yard line. He threw, but he didn't have time to see if Kevin caught the pass. The two mountains collided with him. He felt the breath forced out of him, and a shooting pain running up his left leg. He grunted as he hit the ground. He heard cheers from the home crowd, but that made no sense, since he was lying on the ground.

He tried to get up, but putting weight on his left leg was unbearable. It brought tears to his eyes. He remembered his grandfather's words about not getting sacked, and now RJ understood why the older man had always preached that. It was the reason why quarterbacks got hurt. RJ tried to make the panic go away, but he was concerned that real damage had been done to his leg.

What if he couldn't play the rest of the season? What if he couldn't play in the bowl game? What if he could never play again? Another wave of panic came over him, and in his confusion, he actually grabbed a player from the other team for support.

Coach and a trainer came running onto the field. RJ didn't remember any whistles being blown to stop play, but one must have gone off if non-players were out there. They both slid their arms under his and helped him off the field. Coach shouted a few orders to the assistants, then helped RJ maneuver into the locker room.

RJ was half-lifted onto a table. A team doctor was on-call, and he came over. They started pulling off his cleats and socks.

Another wave of panic surged through his entire body as more sharp pain came from his ankle and foot. Next, the doctor moved the foot to one side, then the other. Twice, RJ cried out in pain, and the doctor stopped to check on the patient. Before starting back the third time, Coach gave RJ a pill to help with the pain. RJ swallowed the pill with a gulp of water and waited. After about 20 minutes, the edge eased off the pain, and better yet, the panic subsided. He rested on the table while the doctor performed the rest of the examination.

RJ could hear the sounds of the stadium above him, but he didn't know who was cheering, or what they were rooting for. He thought about Mya, who had to be worried by this point. He wondered if she would be admitted to the locker room if she asked.

RJ grunted again as the doctor did something to his ankle. He looked down to see a brace and a wrap on it. "The good news is that you only have a sprain. You'll be feeling better in no time."

RJ didn't like the way that this conversation was going. "What's the bad news?"

"You won't be able to play next week, and the week after that will be iffy. We'll just have to see how it goes."

Coach looked at RJ with concern. They both knew what it meant. They'd be relying on a backup quarterback for the game next week, which could affect their overall record and their chance for a bowl game. "Any possibility that you can patch him up before then?" Coach asked. "Can he be exercising or doing any kind of work to get better faster?"

The doctor gave them a wan smile. "Nothing but rest will make him better. If you can handle it, ice it every two hours. If not, do it as much as you can to get the swelling down. If he works it too hard, he'll end up making it worse. He needs to stay off of it as much as possible. I'll put him on crutches for the next week, and add some rehab and physical therapy to work on it. Don't worry. I see these all the time, and they end up fine. This is an inconvenience, not a death sentence."

RJ nodded, trying to look at the bright side of the situation. For a week, he'd just be a normal college student. He'd go to classes, eat dinner, come home, and study. The pills had definitely taken effect, because he was already calm and relaxed. "Fine, I can do this for a week."

The coach handed him a pair of crutches. It took about 15 minutes for RJ to master them. He was slowed down by the pills. He could almost feel them making him move in slow motion. A part of him liked the slowed feeling, since he could just stop and enjoy things. He'd been working so hard for what he wanted that he'd almost forgotten the pleasures of taking it easy.

The doctor handed RJ a bottle of pills as well. "Take these as needed. No more than one every four hours until the pain subsides. After that, you might want to take one before you go to the first few sessions of PT. It will take the edge off any pain you experience."

RJ nodded and stuffed the bottle into his sleeve. He didn't have any pockets at the moment, and maneuvering his way over to his locker seemed like more trouble than it was worth.

Coach led him to the exit. "We really need to get back out there. The fans are going to want to see that you're okay, and you'll want the media to report that you're just banged up. I'll pick a network and have them do a quick interview. Then they can report that you'll be as good as new in a week or two. I don't want rumors getting started, and I know for a fact that you don't want that either."

Mya greeted him at the door of the locker room, her face clearly showed her concern. She looked him up and down, then gave him a hug. "Baby, I was so worried about you. What happened?"

Coach did the explaining, since RJ was still thinking slowly. RJ gave her a smile, then pulled her into a hug. They held each other for a moment, and Coach cleared his throat. "Come on. You have a whole week off to do that. Right now, we have to go out there and make sure that they know you're okay."

RJ gradually made his way out to the benches. A few of the other players raised an eyebrow at the sight of RJ on crutches.

"It's just a sprain," Coach kept saying. "Nothing to worry about."

RJ grinned and heavily sat down on the bench. He nearly nodded off while he was sitting there. That wouldn't do.

No media interview could spare his image if he fell off the bench. So he sat up straight and looked at the score. State was winning by seven.

"How did that happen?" RJ asked no one in particular.

"Kevin caught that pass you threw. We're up, and it's been a stalemate since then," said someone behind him.

RJ nodded. At least the injury had won them the game. He was glad for that much. Coach handed RJ a cellphone. "It's your grandfather. He wants to talk to you."

Taken aback, RJ answered the phone. He told Grandpa that he was fine, just shook up with a slight sprain. He considered this conversation a rehearsal for the media interview. Feeling less nervous now, and hung up after a few reassurances.

State won the game, with neither team scoring again after the pass to Kevin. True to his word, Coach arranged a quick interview with NBC News, and assured everyone that RJ would be fine and playing again soon. Coach implied that the quarterback would be ready for the game next week, which was a surprise. But he played along with Coach's statements.

Mya waited for him after the interview. RJ didn't bother with a shower. The thought of taking off the wrap and splint would be too much for him. Later, he'd find a plastic bag to put around the wrap, so he could shower without taking it off.

Mya spent the night, but they might as well have left the sock off the doorknob. The pain pills apparently decreased his interest in sex. She left the next morning, only after he assured her twenty times that he'd be fine in a few days.

After she left, RJ collapsed on the bed, and wondered what he'd do with a free week to himself.

Chapter 10

THE TRANSITION TO just being a student was eased by the fact that RJ's mother immediately made reservations at a local hotel and drove to State. *Not a motel, but a hotel,* RJ thought. He wondered where that cash had come from, then he realized that his mother was more indebted to the boosters than ever. But his emotions were tempered by the pills he had to take—which made him feel at peace with the world, but very drowsy.

He kept up with what was going on with the team through Kevin and Coach. Kevin gave him a rundown of Sunday's practice. RJ hadn't even bothered to learn the name of the backup quarterback, who'd fumbled twice and thrown two interceptions. Kevin wasn't happy with the situation, and RJ knew that he had to get well, and soon.

Monday had been a blur. His mother managed to call his professors and tell them that RJ would be out of commission for a few days. RJ was glad to hear that none of them assumed that his injury was severe. Apparently, Coach's statement had really placated the press.

His mother had spent the rest of the day running out for RJ's favorite fast foods (which he hadn't had in weeks) and doing laundry. RJ was glad that he didn't have to use his ankle, except for reconditioning activities. His mother had driven him to the physical therapist, who worked his ankle over before sending him back home. He'd barely made it through the door before he went for two more pills.

RJ wished he could have managed the stairs to see his mother in the communal laundry room. Some of his teammates stripped before they did laundry, so they could even wash the clothes they were wearing. He could just imagine how his mother would react: indifferent to all of them, except her baby.

The pain had begun to subside by Tuesday. RJ still had to use crutches to get around campus. He was surprised about how much his arms ached by the end of the day. He thought of himself as an incredible athlete, but he felt like a first-time lifter after a day of crutching around campus. He was late to class twice, because he had to take the elevators, which were ridiculously out of the way. His professor didn't even say anything when he nearly dozed off in English class.

Fortunately, Tuesday's schedule was lighter than his Monday/Wednesday/Friday classes. So RJ was finished by 3:30, and fell asleep while waiting for the other players to come back to the dorm for dinner. He didn't have any homework that night, so it was no big deal that he nearly slept through dinner and crashed again after eating. He was just pleased that he was able to hobble around his room without crutches. He definitely felt the sprain when he put his weight on it, but by walking slowly, he could limp without too much trouble.

The therapist was happy with his progress. During Tuesday's session, Coach had come in twice to see how he was feeling, and what the prospects for Saturday looked like. He was clearly anxious about playing with a backup quarterback, even if they were only playing Mississippi State, who was missing two of its star players at the moment. RJ wondered if MSU was saying the same thing about State.

The therapist appeared positive about the weekend's prospects. RJ was still rather surprised by this optimistic approach. He hadn't practiced all week, and could barely walk normally. And he would be expected to run, pivot, and move side-to-side. The mere thought made his ankle ache.

Wednesday brought more trouble when RJ overslept. He wasn't terribly concerned about it, because his mother had gotten him a reprieve for his philosophy class through Friday. However, their course management system indicated that there was a five-page paper due next Monday, leaving RJ less than a week to complete it.

Then, due to a heating malfunction, his history class was moved to another building. RJ had been late to that class as well. Of course, the trip to the other building, the use of the elevators, and the long walks to the classroom made him ache. He wanted nothing more than to go lie down, but he couldn't. Another history test was scheduled for the following Wednesday, which meant that he had more studying to do.

As he was practicing a pivot, Kevin came back to the room. The pain was nearly unbearable.

"How does that feel?" Kevin said, leaning his head sideways to watch RJ try another pivot. "Looks kind of painful."

"It is," RJ grunted between moves. It was worse than painful. RJ stopped and took two pain pills. Now he'd be asleep in a few minutes, and he couldn't complete any of his assignments if he was snoring.

He pondered another night of crashing out, then not being able to wake up the next morning. He'd have another day of dozing off in class, and not being able to complete the assigned homework. "Hey, can you get me more of that stuff?"

Kevin furrowed his brow. "What stuff? You've got the good stuff already. You don't need anything stronger than Percocet."

"Not that, the stuff to keep you awake. "RJ mimed a good sniff, letting Kevin know what he was talking about.

"Oh yeah, that stuff. Sure, I can get you some. Why? I'd be relieved to be able to take it easy and rest. I'd love to have a hall pass for getting out of practice for one night." Kevin's face broke out into a grin, thinking about a free evening.

"Yeah, well, you don't have a paper due and a test next week," RJ said, propping his foot up on a pillow. "I need to put in some serious study time."

"Actually, I do have a test, but it'll go on without me." Kevin shrugged, pulled out his phone, and texted someone. In a few seconds, the phone chirped, and he checked his screen. "I'll have the stuff after dinner. Then you can get in some study time tonight. I got to tell you, wanting to study in college is way more subversive than taking drugs."

RJ laughed and nodded. He felt his eyes grow heavy, and he fell asleep again.

When he awoke two hours later, there was a Post-it note on his forehead saying: "The stuff's under your pillow." RJ reached his arm around and felt under the pillow. Kevin had been good to his word. RJ did as Kevin had shown him before: He took out a pill, crushed it, and sniffed the remains. In moments, his head was clear.

He managed to get out of bed. Even his ankle felt better with the drugs. He used his crutches to walk across the room, and sat down to start working on the paper. Now he could focus on the project.

He skipped dinner, opting for a quick snack from the machines in the hallway. He returned to his room. He shook his head, thinking about Kevin. How could he not worry about his grades? RJ knew he couldn't live with himself if he failed a class. Not after his family had sacrificed so much. He really only had one chance to get this right.

By the time he finished the paper, it was nearly 11 pm. RJ looked around the room, wanting to do something else. He was wired now, and he didn't want to sleep. It felt like he'd been sleeping for days. He thought about cleaning or doing laundry, but his mother had done all of that. He eyed his bed. Maybe sleep was the best thing for him.

Yet he didn't feel sleepy. He hadn't been this awake in days. He dropped to the bed and twisted his body around so that he was lying down. His eyes were wide open, and he knew sleep wouldn't come.

After a few minutes of trying to rest, RJ found the bottle of Percocet and took two of them. It had been more than the prescribed time, so he wasn't worried about an overdose. It should just allow him to fall asleep when he needed to.

The following morning, he awoke with only ten minutes left before class started. He cursed the pain pills, and hopped around the room to get into sweats and a t-shirt. On crutches, no one expected too much from his wardrobe, so he was fine. He was still dragging as he got ready to leave. He just couldn't do it again today. He had another visit with the physical therapist, who would ask how he was doing. RJ wanted to be able to tell him that he was doing better.

The pills that Kevin had gotten for him were just what he needed to get through the day. He took another pill, crushed it, and sniffed it. By the time RJ hit the quad, he was feeling like he'd never been injured. The pills were that good. He still used the crutches, but the ankle didn't hurt like it had. He barely thought of it as he worked through English that day.

A few times that day, he still used the crutches. And he'd found himself feeling constrained by them. He wanted his arms to move faster, so that he could get where he wanted to be. He'd felt somewhat resigned to using the crutches before, yet now he was anxious to be done with them. He talked to his PT that day about getting around without them.

The therapist noticed the difference in his mood. "You seem more upbeat than you have the last few days," he said, watching RJ's reaction to the different exercises.

"I'm feeling better than I was," RJ replied. "I think it just needed time."

"The body is a wonderful thing, and it can perform miracles if left on its own," the therapist said. "You just can't rush it."

RJ frowned. "What are you saying?"

"I think that you need to sit this game out."

The words hit him like a 300-pound linebacker. He'd never been out for an injury before, and he didn't want to start now. The words of the agent rushed over him. What would happen to his chances of going pro this year if he sat out a game? Would teams still be interested in him, or would they make him defer his dream for another year? He couldn't imagine going another year of long hours and penny-pinching. He suddenly found himself very weary, as if all of the sacrifices and scrimping had suddenly caught up with him. He didn't want to wait for his dreams to come true. He wanted them now.

"Is that necessary? Couldn't I play part of the game?"

Now the therapist frowned. "You could, but you could also reinjure yourself and aggravate a simple sprain into something more. I know you don't want that. The team doesn't want that, and the coach doesn't want that. They all want a healthy quarterback."

RJ grew angry. He didn't want to wait. He knew it was important to heal, but it was also important to play. This man was talking about RJ's future without knowing all the facts. The therapist would still have his crappy job here, no matter what happened on Saturday.

"How are you doing with the pain pills? Do you need more?" the therapist asked, obviously trying to change the subject.

"No, I'm good," RJ said. Now he didn't want to get any more meds, thinking it might be seen as a sign of weakness. He couldn't have that if he wanted to play on Saturday. They had to view him as healed and healthy.

When RJ returned to his dorm room, he threw the crutches on the bed. If he was going to play on Saturday, they were going to be permanently retired. He knew that nothing screamed "not ready" like hobbling around on crutches.

He tentatively walked around the room, and the ankle held. It wasn't hurting too bad, despite the therapy. RJ wasn't sure if Kevin's drugs were the cause of the improvement, or if he was really feeling better. But he didn't care. He was putting the same drive and single-mindedness that had gotten him this far to work on his ankle. He was going to play, and he was going to get into the NFL this year. It was merely a matter of mind over body.

RJ tried to study for his test, but his eyes kept wandering back to the agents' folders on his desk. At one point, he picked one up again and skimmed through the pages. His imagination replaced the stars' faces with his own. He liked the way it looked. He liked the cars, the women, and the homes.

He had only managed about ten minutes of real studying by the time he went out to dinner. He took a history book with him to study, but he only read a few pages. His mind returned to the agent's folder.

When he got back to the dorm room, Kevin was there. He was obviously getting ready for a night out. "Look at you: no crutches. Does that mean you're going to be able to play on Saturday?"

RJ shrugged, hoping that his resolve didn't show too clearly. He didn't want to be suspected of powering through an injury, so that his coach would keep him out of the game. He knew that Coach only had his best interests at heart, but there was no way he could know the pressures that RJ was under.

Coach had been there forever. Short of going 0-10, Coach was practically guaranteed a job through retirement. He already knew what he was going to be doing next month and next year. The opponents and bowl games might change, but Coach was settled. RJ still had all of that in front of him, and nothing was settled for him. It could all go his way, or could all turn to nothing.

"Yeah, I hope you can. I'm hearing that one of their players who's been out is coming back for the game against State. Since you're supposed to be out, they're pushing him to play."

"Great," RJ replied. Nothing like a little more pressure to heal faster. "If things keep going well, I should be able to play on Saturday."

Kevin slapped him on the shoulder. "Dude, that calls for a celebration. You got to come out with us tonight."

RJ hadn't thought about going out. He should be studying for his test. However, the pressures that had been building up inside his head made him crave some kind of release. *Everyone needs to blow off steam,* he thought. *Why not me?*

"Sure. Let me get ready."

Kevin stared at him. "Dude, that was way too easy. I expected that I'd have to lift you out of your chair and drag you to a bar. Instead, you're all agreeable."

RJ shrugged. "I need a break. I've been studying a lot lately." That statement was *almost* true. He'd been *trying* to study a lot lately.

RJ looked at his phone for a moment. Mya was supposed to call that night, but RJ's battery was nearly dead. He'd have to leave it on the charger, so he'd miss her call.

He rationalized that there would always be other times. For the first time, RJ noticed how much more relaxed he was about things. He had no issues with partying. He could miss a call from his girl. Was he just getting to the point where he needed to get away, or was this a side effect of the pills?

To be honest, RJ had no idea which one of the medications made him feel this way. While trying to handle the demands of school and football, he'd been taking them one after the other. He couldn't keep them all straight at this point.

They went up to the same bar, McCabe's, and found the same table. RJ actually liked that Kevin could be a creature of habit, even if they only represented bad habits. He still didn't know all that much about his roommate, even though they'd been sharing a room for nearly three months. It was odd how cutoff RJ had felt from Kevin.

But tonight, he felt like they were really friends. Of course, the feeling of comradery could have been due to the alcohol.

Kevin actually stopped RJ after his second beer, telling him to take it easy, since he was on meds. "They can have some bad side effects, dude. You don't want that." RJ was touched that Kevin was concerned enough to care about his health. But then he had a moment of doubt, since Kevin's future was tied to a good season for State. But he let the thought go and watched the bodies shaking on the dance floor.

"You want to dance?" Kevin asked him. "Go." He gave RJ a push toward the dance floor.

RJ nearly returned to his seat. But after a few girls moved in his direction, he followed along. The music was playing a pop song that RJ didn't recognize. An easygoing mood washed over him again, and he didn't care how he looked dancing. He stood in one place, mainly to keep down the wear on his ankle, but he danced and enjoyed himself.

He felt awkward as he stood there, so he waved his arms in the air. Just then, two girls came up and starting dancing with him. And the self-consciousness left him as they swayed. One of the girls moved closer and pressed her body against his. His body started to react to her before he realized what he was doing. He mumbled something to her, then quickly shuffled off the floor.

What was I thinking? What would Mya say if she saw me dancing like that with someone else? He shuddered, thinking about how his body had betrayed him so easily.

He vowed that he would get off these pills. They weakened all of his resolve—from studying to drinking to straying from Mya. Though he liked the way they made the pain go away, he wasn't about to gain an NFL career, but lose everything else that mattered to him.

Kevin looked at him. "Dude, you had two girls all over you, and you walked away. Forget MVP. You should get Saint of the Year for that one." He laughed as he looked over at the two girls, who were still dancing. One of them waved at Kevin.

"You know I'm not going to mess things up with Mya." Now RJ knew that he definitely had to get off these pills, and soon. That had been too close. He knew that he wouldn't want Mya dancing with other guys, so he held himself to that same standard.

"That's cool." Kevin flashed a smile at one of the girls. "Hey, would you be upset if I took those ladies home with me?"

RJ laughed. "No, go right ahead. I think I'm going to go to the library."

Kevin looked at him with disgust. "Now? What happened to Fun RJ? I was liking him."

"I have a history test that I need to study for," RJ said as he threw a couple of dollars on the table as a tip. "Don't worry. I'll be gone before you get home, and I won't be home until late. The room is all yours."

Kevin gave him a light punch on the arm. "I can leave one in your bed for you if you want. I can wear her out so bad that she won't be able to walk."

RJ shook his head. First he headed to the dorm, then to the library. There, he found a table and pulled out his history books. At 2 am, he was still buzzed from the ADHD meds. He wasn't going to take anything else to make him sleep.

He knew that he'd pay for this tomorrow, but he didn't care. He had to work his way back to being whole again. It was worth it, and it was right. He didn't care how hard it was, or how much pain he was in. He'd worked hard before, and he'd hurt before.

RJ considered talking to his grandfather about everything. He missed his advice, but it was clear that the older man didn't know how to maneuver a college-level game. He'd even seen him with Edward Donley, which wasn't a good choice at all. So RJ felt the need to handle this situation on his own.

By the time he made it home from the library, Kevin was already asleep. RJ slid into bed, but he was still wired from the pills. He was very tempted to take a Percocet, but he knew he'd have to come down from it eventually. So it might as well be now.

Chapter 11

THE NEXT MORNING, RJ hit the dining hall and had several cups of coffee. He had a meeting with Coach after class to see how he felt—and finally decide whether or not he'd play the following day. He headed off to his first class of the day, but one of his agents was outside the dining hall: the ex-football player with the florid face. "Hey kid, I know you were up late last night. Saw you at the bar. I thought you could use this."

RJ was ready to be handed pills or illegal drugs, but the man just handed him a large black coffee from Starbucks. He took a long sip. "Thanks. I'm on my way to class now."

"I know. English. For a first-year quarterback, you're taking on a pretty ambitious schedule. I want to tell you that if you decide to go pro before you're out of college, we'd put some sort of package together. Then you could either finish your degree during the off-season or after you finish your career. You seem to be the type who wants to better himself."

RJ nodded. "Yeah, my parents sacrificed a lot to get me here. I don't want to waste any opportunity to get ahead."

"Admirable. So what are they saying about your ankle? Is it looking like you'll play this weekend?"

RJ was walking without his crutches, but anyone could see that his ankle was still bothering him a little. He walked deliberately, taking each step with care. "I'm hoping to play tomorrow. I heard that MSU is putting one of their players back in because they're thinking I'll sit it out."

The man laughed. "Don't listen to the rumors, kid. They'll lead you in the wrong direction. Both Lamar and Jesse are out for at least two more weeks. See, this is one of the things that agents can help with. I have sources that you'll never meet, and they tell me things that you'll never hear. Lamar is out for at least two weeks. Then he'll likely be back. If Jesse comes back on the third week, he'll be pushing it. Their coach is pushing it, too, but that's not a good thing for the kid. He could end up with permanent damage, and destroy any chance of a pro career."

RJ listened and nodded. It was good to know this. It took a little pressure off of him to play the next day. But he still wanted to do his best for the team and his chances at the NFL.

"So here's my recommendation: Stay off it for another week. Do the therapy, take the pills, and come back next week for the game against Sedona Falls. State's not going to have a problem with MSU, in the shape it's in. So take the opportunity to rest some more."

RJ appreciated the man's comments. Since he'd learned that his grandfather wasn't able to answer questions at the college level, he'd felt somewhat rudderless. Even if he was only hoping to make money off of RJ, it still made sense to him. RJ realized that the man might want him to be a long-term client, which meant that he'd vie for RJ to be healthy and productive in both college and the NFL. That counted for something.

As RJ walked slowly to the elevator in the English building, he realized that he hadn't even thought about the fact that the coffee was technically a gift, which should have been returned. Given his near-indiscretion at the bar, he was again concerned that the pills had made his resolve weak.

With some counsel about what to do, RJ's classes flew by. He turned in his paper early, and he felt relatively confident about the test when he saw the study guide that the TA gave him. By the time that he'd made it to the practice field, he was feeling good. Coach waved at him and started walking toward him.

He warmly greeted RJ. "Hey kid, how are you feeling?"

"Pretty good, but still not all the way," RJ honestly replied. "Therapy is working it, but I'm still limping a little. I'm not sure what to do about tomorrow's game."

Coach nodded. "How do you feel on those painkillers that you got?"

"Kind of sleepy. Not really all there. I fell asleep at 7 pm one night." RJ watched Coach's reaction carefully, trying to understand what he was getting at. Was he suggesting that he should take pills before the game? That would be worse than not playing at all. His motor skills would be too far out of whack to consider all the possibilities.

"Tell you what. I'm a little iffy about playing you tomorrow. The Sedona Falls game is crucial."

RJ nodded. He'd heard the rumors about some of the faculty and the major donors betting on the game. He knew there was pressure to win at all costs.

"So I'm going to have you suit up tomorrow for the game. That ought to put a little scare into MSU. But I won't have you play unless it's crucial that our best player be out there for us. Does that sound good?"

RJ agreed. It was a strategy that went just beyond what the agent had said. State would beat MSU without its two players handy, so why waste RJ on that game when he was needed the following week?

Coach walked back out to the field, and RJ made his way into the PT room. The therapist wasn't there, so he just sat and thought about what had just happened: *How does Coach know that this is the best thing for me? He really doesn't. He echoed the agent, to some degree. But both of them are looking out for other things, not me. So how much do I trust Coach with my future—my family's future?*

He was still thinking about this situation when the therapist came in. He made RJ go through a litany of new exercises. By the time they were done, RJ wished he'd brought his crutches to the training room. His ankle was throbbing.

"Do you have something else for the pain?" RJ asked. "I don't want to get hooked on any kind of pain medication, you know?"

The therapist nodded. "I can give you something else, but to be honest, that's the best one for pain. I know they're addictive. I monitor every athlete that I give the meds to. I didn't think I had to be as worried about you. You always seem to have everything together."

"They just make me sleepy," RJ said, thinking of his early nights. "Then I almost feel hungover the next morning."

"I'm not going to ask how you know what hungover feels like," the therapist said with a smile. "But I understand what you're talking about. You're not the only one to complain about them. You can always break them in half if you need to. You'll get half of the benefits, but also half of the side effects."

RJ nodded. After the therapy session, he had a quick bite to eat in the dining hall and went back to his room to study. The pain started to bother him, but with tomorrow's game, RJ opted to power through. He didn't want to be messed up during the game in any way.

The game with MSU turned out better than RJ expected. The crowd was nearly as large as some of the first games of the season. Fans were starting to smell a bowl game, and they came back to the stands to be able to say that they'd followed the season.

As the agent predicted, neither of the MSU players were on the roster for the game. Coach still had RJ suit up, but he sat on the bleachers for most of the first half. RJ still couldn't get used to being on the sidelines. His parents hadn't called at all this week to say they'd miss the game. And RJ avoided the call from his grandfather. Mya had asked about coming. But he pointed out that he wouldn't be doing anything, and he still had a test to study for.

In the fourth quarter, Coach had RJ run three plays, just to get him out there. The fans went crazy, shouting and whooping to see him back on the field. RJ was touched by the adoration. He knew that the coach had done it to buoy his spirits, which had been down that week.

RJ realized how much the school liked him, and he began to question whether he should leave at the end of his freshman year. If he had three more years of this type of support, he'd be a fool to abandon it, only to possibly fail in the pros. Yet he was still drawn in by the money. It always came back to the money.

At the end of the third play, his ankle had begun to protest. He made a signal to Coach, who pulled him out of the game. He limped off to the sidelines and sat down. The pain grew with each passing minute, and RJ knew that he'd have to use the pain pills again. Fortunately, he had nothing due the next day, so it would be alright.

The game finished with State winning 30-7. RJ skipped all the post-game celebrations and hurried back to his room to get a pain pill. He gulped it down with water, then relaxed on the bed with his foot propped up. He must have dozed off quickly—because the next thing he knew, Kevin was back in the room with a girl.

"Hey, RJ. Can you find something to do? I have someone to do here." He smacked the girl on the butt and smiled at his roommate.

"I'll go get a bite at the dining hall."

Kevin shook his head. "Sorry, bro. It's closed. It's almost 8:30."

RJ looked around, trying to think of what to do. Since no one had been to see him this week, his wallet was empty.

Kevin must have figured out that RJ was broke, so he pushed the leather portfolio toward him. "Give him a call. He'll take you out to dinner at a nice restaurant."

RJ was still groggy, so he did as Kevin suggested. The agent agreed to pick him up at the dorm and take him to dinner. By the time RJ used the elevator to get downstairs, the agent was sitting at the curb in a BMW.

"Get in, kid. Where do you want to go?"

RJ shrugged. He honestly didn't even know the names of any good restaurants in town. If it wasn't fast food, RJ had no idea what to pick.

The agent sighed. "We'll go to Ruth's Chris. Can't go wrong there."

RJ settled back in his seat and nestled into the leather. Before he knew it, the agent stopped the car. RJ had never even heard of Ruth's Chris before. According to the number of Lexuses, BMWs, and Jaguars in the parking lot, RJ figured that he hadn't heard of it because it was out of his price range. Maybe when he was pulling in the big bucks, he'd bring his whole family here for dinner.

After they ordered, the waitress offered him a drink menu. But RJ refused, thinking about what Kevin had told him about drug interactions. He didn't want anyone—especially an agent—intimating that he had addiction issues before he was even drafted. He asked for water, and the agent, seemingly following his lead, asked for iced tea.

"Glad to see that you didn't overdo today. Next week is a big game, and you'll want to be in tip-top shape by then."

"Do you think I'll be ready?" RJ asked, still in a lot of pain.

"You'll need to be. I have some people coming in next week to see you play. We're talking about people who can make or break your career. I want them to see what I've seen." The agent took a sip of his iced tea and made a face. RJ suspected that he typically made deals over drinks a lot stronger than that.

"I'll do what I can." RJ thought of his plays in the next week's game. He hoped he'd be able to perform with his ankle.

The waiter returned and took their order. RJ had ordered a 20 oz porterhouse. He didn't even know what cut of steak that was, but it sounded fancy.

As they were chatting, Coach and some of his assistants came into the restaurant. Coach didn't say a word to RJ, but there was condemnation in his gaze, reminding him not to get involved with agents who only wanted him to go pro as soon as he could. Did this agent want short-term profits, or a long-term career?

After that, RJ didn't enjoy the meal as much. Of course, the steak was incredible. RJ knew he hadn't had a cut of beef that good in ages, certainly not since he'd been at State. Yet the coach's occasional glances to his table made him uneasy. Would he get reported to the NCAA for accepting a meal? He remembered the shoes from the beginning of the year. They seemed to have the stamp of approval from Coach, so maybe everything could still work out okay.

After dinner, he popped another pain pill. Sitting upright with his leg underneath him made his ankle swell, and the pain thumped in his foot.

"Still bothering you?" the agent asked.

"Yeah." RJ said. Now he just wished he was home in bed.

"Just don't get too dependent on those pills. I've seen sprains and fractures lead to full-blown drug abuse. The pressure is a lot to bear, so some people seek an easy way out. I don't want that happening to you."

RJ nodded. He had no desire to get addicted either. He just wanted to heal and play football.

The agent signaled for the waiter, handed him a credit card, and smiled at RJ. "I don't have to tell you that your coach is here. It's not a big thing. If he reported everyone he saw having a meal with me, he would have to forfeit, due to a lack of players. I just forgot that he likes to come here after games to relax."

RJ doubted that. He figured that the agent knew where Coach went for dinner, and wanted to display a bit of ownership over RJ. He knew he'd been right not to trust an agent with his future.

RJ dozed most of the way home. The agent pulled up in front of the dorm. He stepped out of the car, gingerly putting pressure on his foot and ankle. The pain was bearable when he was on these pills.

He crashed out on his bed, and didn't wake up until nearly noon the next day. *Damn.* He wanted to be up early and get some more studying done. He ate a small brunch. He could still taste that incredible steak from last night. He realized what a constant stream of low-quality meals he was being fed here.

RJ grew annoyed again. While he was making millions for State and the NCAA, he was still trying to make his meal ticket last all semester. He put the thoughts out of his mind as best he could, and began studying for the test again.

He hadn't seen Kevin since the evening before, but that was okay. He was getting a lot done in the room, where he could put his foot up and occasionally ice it. He took pain pills as he needed them and studied some more.

He must have fallen asleep again, as he awoke to Kevin reading and listening to his beats. RJ went back to studying, and tried to ignore his roommate. RJ wasn't sure how he could process the text while listening to another set of words. He knew that Kevin mostly had easy classes, which required very little reading comprehension.

After his last set of pills, RJ slept through the night. He woke up the next morning, feeling sluggish and out of sorts. He thought about all of the warnings he'd heard recently from the PT, from the agent, even from Kevin. Nevertheless, he wanted that feeling back.

So he reached under his pillow for one of the ADHD pills that Kevin had procured for him. He crushed it and sniffed it. The high was almost immediate. RJ showered, dressed, and walked to his English class—all without pain. By the time he got there, he was feeling pretty invincible. He was going to be okay for Sedona Falls after all.

A new TA passed out the papers, and RJ couldn't believe his grade. He'd received a D. The comments reflected that he'd done a much better job on his philosophy paper. *The one he hadn't written*, RJ thought. He only had one more paper to write, and his average was still above a C. So he would be fine. He took a deep breath, but the positive feelings were gone.

He managed the next two days without any major issues. The history exam wasn't as bad as he thought. He felt he'd done well, but those doubts from the English paper nagged at him. What if he only thought he'd done well? What if he'd actually bombed the test? RJ could barely get through the rest of the day.

Then he started panicking about the exam and the paper and everything else school-related. Were the pressures getting to him? Did everyone know that he was muddling through with the help of pills?

He wished he hadn't listened to his parents about taking a full course load while playing football. They'd both gone to college. Why didn't they tell him about all of the pressures that awaited him here? Didn't they know?

RJ called Mya for the third time that week. She'd been incredibly patient with all of his concerns. But he didn't tell her about the ADHD pills, since she wouldn't understand. She'd lost an uncle to heroin, and she was adamant that she'd never be involved with a drug user. RJ was worried that he'd be "a drug user" in her eyes, so she'd break up with him. He knew that some things were non-negotiable with her. As much as they loved each other, she would never put herself through what she'd seen her aunt go through with her uncle.

Based on her experience, he honestly thought she'd more easily forgive him for sleeping with someone else than doing drugs.

After they got off the phone, RJ decided to take a walk. He was strung out from everything he'd done that week, and he felt adrift—like he didn't have a purpose. Even though he knew exactly where he was going, he felt like missing most of the MSU game and eating with the agent had sidetracked him. RJ wished he could get the resolve back that he had when he first started college.

Even though he hadn't snorted any ADHD pills, he noticed that his ankle felt better. He was able to walk around campus without pain.

After RJ told Coach, he made him go through a series of tests, just to show that he was able to bend it and run without experiencing pain. He'd never bounced so much in his life.

On Thursday, Coach announced that RJ was ready to play on Saturday. It had been long enough. Kevin insisted on a celebration after practice. RJ agreed to go for one drink, not wanting to get too into the scene that Kevin enjoyed so much.

They went to another bar this time, which some of his teammates said was rowdier than McCabe's. And they were right. Just to order drinks, they had to yell at the bartender. After the third round of shots, RJ felt a buzz. Who had he been kidding, thinking that he'd actually get out of there after just one drink?

Kevin went out to dance. When two girls waved at RJ, he waved back to be polite. Then they approached RJ. The blonde girl leaned in close to his ear, and told him that Kevin wanted him out on the dance floor. In the dim lights of the club, the other one appeared to be Latina. She tugged on RJ's hand as they headed to the floor.

Kevin was dancing the best he could, but he looked more out of it than usual. RJ wondered if he'd been doing drugs, in addition to drinking. Then Kevin stumbled and nearly fell onto the floor. The two girls helped him stand up.

RJ threw Kevin's arm over his shoulder and helped him back to the table. The added weight of his roommate made his ankle hurt a little. He nearly tripped over a piece of loose carpet as well, which only made the pain worse. RJ grew anxious, thinking that he'd be unable to play on Saturday.

At the table, RJ pawned Kevin off on one of the other guys. He wanted to pay the tab, but he knew there wasn't enough money in his account. He ended up fishing Kevin's wallet out of his pocket and paying with his card.

They made for the door and headed back to the dorm. Out in the night air, RJ was able to assess his ankle. It wasn't bad. He'd just frozen up, worrying about damaging it further. His concern was understandable. If he was out another two or three weeks and missed the Sedona Falls game, he could possibly be watching State play at a bowl game from his dorm room.

Chapter 12

THE GAME DAY was cold and dreary. The dampness made RJ's ankle feel a little stiff. So he went and did his PT exercises bright and early, which made his ankle more flexible. Then he ate an early breakfast. None of the other team members were up yet, so he ate in silence. The thought that it had been two weeks since he'd played an entire game for State made him nervous. He felt like he was playing in the Youth League for the first time, rather than at the college level.

RJ opted to call his grandfather before the game. During his time off, he hadn't talked to him directly. He didn't want to disappoint him with the news that he was taking a week off. Grandpa was old school. Men didn't skip games. They powered through, no matter what. He probably would have told Joe Theismann to play through his open fracture.

"Have you been following what the therapist told you to do?" his grandfather asked, almost sounding rational about missing a game.

"Yeah, definitely. Nothing fancy, you know. No marathons or lifting cars."

"Good, you should do what they tell you. They'll get you healed, so you can play. I trust that coach to do the best thing for you."

RJ paused at those words. His grandfather's tone was different. He sounded rehearsed, unnatural. For a minute, he wondered if Grandpa's new friend, Edward Donley, had coerced him into saying these words.

"I trust Coach, too." Then RJ changed the subject and talked about State's possible bowl games. They spoke for almost 45 minutes before RJ looked at the clock. Then he realized that he'd have to go soon, in order to make it to the locker room in time to prep.

They hung up, and RJ thought about his grandfather's words again. Grandpa had always regarded himself as RJ's best source of advice, and now he'd suddenly deferred to Coach. RJ was suspicious of the change.

Despite it being the biggest game of the season, his parents opted not to come. His mother had a deadline that she had to meet, and of course, RJ's father offered no excuse. Mya said that she might come down if she could get a ride. One of the guys from her computer class was a

State fan, and he wanted to go to the game. RJ felt a bit jealous of this new friend. He kept telling himself that Mya loved him and wanted to be with him, but it had been weeks since they'd seen each other. The last time they'd been together, he was in too much pain to make love. *Did she start seeing this guy? Is there something going on with them?*

RJ pushed all the thoughts out of his head as he entered the locker room. At that moment, he was all about the game. He'd contemplate these other things later, once he'd gotten this game over with and proved to himself that he was still able to perform.

When the team ran out on the field, RJ was stunned at the size of the crowd. It was by far the biggest one of the year. The stadium was packed. The student section had spilled over—to the point that they sat on the ground and under the stands. As RJ ran to his team's position on the sidelines, the noise was deafening. He waved at the crowd, then focused on the game.

Coach reminded him that Sedona Falls had a great passing defense. Given his ankle injury, they'd be expecting RJ to pass as much as possible. They'd expect him to want to keep clear of any interaction with the other team, so that he could stay on his feet and not get hit again. RJ and Coach had gone over several plays that would allow them to run the ball without putting undue pressure on RJ to run it himself. Coach stressed that he should not test his ankle and see if he could run the length of the field.

RJ came out for the first play of the game, and the crowds went wild. The stomping of the students on the stands made the field slightly quake. RJ felt a surge of enjoyment from the adulation. He followed Coach's playbook, ran three downs, and only advanced seven yards. The defense came out, and the stands grew quiet.

"I told you: They're a tough team. Don't underestimate what they can do. They'll shut you down without a yard if they can." Coach put a hand on RJ's back, and tried to make him feel better about the weak yardage.

The first half played out the same way. No matter what play RJ ran, Sedona Falls' defense shut him down. He'd only managed 45 yards in the first half, which put him on track to score less than 100 yards of passing and rushing in the game. It was an all-time low for him.

The team seemed very somber as they went into the locker room. Coach gave them a rousing speech that was supposed to inspire them. RJ heard the words but didn't feel any enthusiasm. He knew that unless something changed, the game would end without State scoring a point.

On their first play of the second half, the same thing happened. RJ despaired that it wasn't going to change. On the next play, he decided to act. His ankle experienced a twinge, but he knew that this game would stay locked at zero otherwise.

RJ took a step back, faked a pass to Kevin, and held onto the ball. Instead, he ran it for 15 yards, then ran out of bounds on the side of the field. The crowds went wild. So did Coach, but for different reasons.

"What the hell were you doing out there? You could have been hurt. You could have gotten sacked. You could have fumbled the ball. This is a team sport, and you decided to make a play that involved only you. Are you playing for the team right now, or are you playing to go to the pros? Which is it, Robinson?"

Coach's face was red and blotched from screaming. RJ took off his helmet, thinking he was going to be benched. But instead, Coach yelled at him for a few more minutes. The ref's whistle blew, and Coach just looked at him.

"Well, we've got us a game to win," he said. "Just don't do any more showboating. I want us to win as a team, and I want you in one piece when we're done."

RJ went back out on the field. The crowd was still going wild, but RJ could hear the taunts from the Sedona Falls players as they lined up for the next play. RJ tried to block out their threats about what they would do to him for that fake.

When the ball snapped, RJ watched around him, the threats still ringing in his ears. He knew that they would break through the line as soon as they could to try and sack him. With that in mind, he threw for a long pass. He hit the player, who caught the ball and ran it in for a touchdown long before any of the Sedona Falls players could get to him.

With the score 7-0 State, RJ took a seat on the bench.

"How's the ankle?" Coach asked, watching RJ as he did some exercises to stay limber.

"It's fine. I'm just a bit nervous after being hit."

"You're being conventional. We're going to have to shake it up if we're going to win." Coach outlined a few plays for them during the second half.

The team seemed reenergized when they took the field again. They made a first down on the first play. They went for another down on the next play. There were no spectacular plays, but they drove the ball far enough down the field that the kicker was able to score, which brought the score to 10-0.

The rest of the game was a stalemate. State won the game and blocked Sedona Falls from scoring. The crowd shouted and hooted so loud that the coach couldn't do an interview on the field. The team headed off to the locker room, and the media followed them.

Coach grabbed RJ by the shoulder and held him back. RJ turned to find several microphones in his face. "What do you think of your bowl chances?"

"Did you think that you'd win today's game?"

RJ did his best. He'd memorized a few pat answers to the questions. And he used the buzzwords that Coach had schooled him in and seen other athletes use during interviews. The media finally seemed satisfied, and RJ headed off to find the rest of the team.

"How's the ankle?" Coach asked as RJ was leaving.

"Doing good. No problems." RJ did a few hops to prove his point.

He quickly changed clothes, knowing that Mya was waiting for him. He told Kevin that Mya was outside, and Kevin nodded, knowing it was his turn to find another place to stay that night.

However, when RJ finally found Mya, she was standing next to a young man and earnestly talking with him. He listened to their conversation for a few minutes, but he didn't have a clue as to what they were talking about. Mya laughed, and RJ saw the man's face light up.

He stepped forward so they could see him. "Hey, baby."

RJ walked closer and leaned down for a kiss. Even though it was a quick peck on the cheek, Mya seemed uncomfortable. Normally, she'd be as happy to see him as he was to see her. But today, it felt like she was holding back.

"RJ, this is Mike. He's a fan."

"Man, am I! You were awesome today. I would have loved to have seen 'The Play.' But I guess with that ankle, a run like that would have been hard to pull off."

RJ just nodded. He wondered if the guy had gotten all of this from the news, or if Mya had been confiding in him. "Yeah, the ankle's doing better. It's just a little tender."

Mike looked down, as if to check out the ankle. "So what are you thinking about your bowl chances?"

He and RJ made small talk about football for a few minutes. Mike did seem to be informed about State, including things that he wouldn't have learned from Mya. In fact, he knew stats for every member of the team, and even information about Coach. RJ didn't realize that Coach had been at State for nearly 25 years. "He should be getting ready for retirement in a few," Mike added. "But who could replace him? He's an institution, like Bear Bryant."

RJ hadn't thought of the future, at least anyone else's. Coach had been great so far, leading him along the path as he tried to figure out what to do and how to recover. Suddenly, RJ felt sad. He realized that Coach might not be around for his entire college career, even if he chose to finish it out.

They stood there and chatted for several more minutes. Even though Mya had already hugged him twice, RJ wanted to go somewhere else, anywhere else, and spend some time alone with her. He'd missed her terribly, and didn't want to spend their entire time with Mike.

Mya cleared her throat. "Baby, I know you don't want to hear this, but I have to go. Mike's driving me, because my car still won't go above 55 mph. I can't stay over, and let him sleep in his car. It wouldn't be right."

RJ tried to force his brain to come up with a solution for Mike, but nothing worked that would leave the man in good circumstances. Except the agent. RJ excused himself from them for a minute. He dialed the agent, who picked up on the second ring.

"Great job in the game today. People are talking about you. A little bit of self-aggrandizement. Isn't that a great word? Sounds so much better than ball hog, but you get the point. Don't do that too often, okay?"

"Yes, sir." RJ explained the situation and asked if he could get a room for Mike for the night.

"Things are kind of crowded. But give me ten, and I'll see what I can do. Deal?"

RJ hung up and went back to the pair. He explained what was going on. Mike seemed a bit embarrassed by the offer, and Mya was surprised. "I thought you weren't allowed to take anything from anyone." Then she fumed. "Even though it's for Mike, you're the one asking for it. I can't let you do this."

Mike looked a little disappointed about missing out on a free hotel room, but Mya motioned for him to come along. And he actually obeyed, like he expected to get rewarded for following her commands. RJ felt jealous and insecure. Had she already passed him up for someone else—someone who didn't bend the rules for the sake of their relationship?

RJ tried to say something to prevent her from leaving, but she cut him off. "RJ, I'm just mad right now. We'll talk this week and get everything straightened out." She gave him another peck on the cheek and got in the car, a multicolored beater that was a world away from the BMW he'd ridden in the other night.

RJ stared at the car as it drove off. *What happened here?* He'd been shot down like a guy asking out a girl for the first time. She was going home with that Mike dude, and he was all alone.

RJ went back to his room alone. Kevin was getting cleaned up. He looked surprised to see RJ alone. "Dude, what happened? I thought you were using the room tonight. I bought some Clorox Wipes to clean up the mess you were gonna make. It's been months since you got any. I figured it would be all over the place." He laughed at his own joke.

"No dice, man. She rode up with some dude from her school, and went home the same way. I didn't even get a proper kiss." RJ tried to think of another time when he'd been this jealous, but he couldn't. Mya had always been there for him.

"Sucks to be you." Kevin slid a shirt over his head. "Anyway, we're all going to the bar tonight. You want to come along?"

RJ looked around the room. There was nothing for him to do there. "Yeah, might as well."

"Alright, man. Now we're talking. We'll be unstoppable tonight at the bar—just like we were on the field."

RJ just rolled his eyes. "Yeah, man, whatever you say."

Kevin broke into a grin. "You got any of those pills left? I could use a hit before we go out."

RJ nodded. What else could he do, since Kevin was the one that gave them to him? He fished them out from under his pillow. Damn, there were only three left. Had Kevin gotten into his stash, or had RJ actually used that many of them himself? The second possibility was startling.

Kevin crushed the pill and scooped up the powder into his palm. He held it out to RJ. "Ladies first," he said with a laugh.

RJ took a healthy sniff and felt the familiar rush. He watched as Kevin did the same. Kevin was suddenly more talkative—laughing and sharing stories. And RJ felt the enjoyment of friendship. He tried to put Mya out of his mind by focusing on the here and now.

Laughing at a joke, they headed to McCabe's, and a group joined them on the way. He recognized two of them as players from the football team. RJ already knew that he'd be counting on others to buy him drinks, because he only had $5 in his wallet.

Sure enough, someone else bought the first round of shots. RJ downed the shot and felt the burn of the liquor down his throat. He wondered what Mya was doing now. *Did she just go home, or did she go somewhere with Mike?* He shook his head, trying to get the negative thoughts out of his head. He didn't want to believe that Mya could like someone else better than him.

Kevin bought the next round: double scotch. The liquor tasted like dirt to him, but Kevin kept urging him to take small sips and forget his problems. RJ definitely wanted to do that, so he kept sipping on it. But RJ couldn't stand the taste anymore, so he just held his nose and downed it. He could feel the rush from the drink, and it was amazing. He felt free from his responsibilities and pressures. He wondered if it was how Kevin felt all the time. Just the good times—and none of the pressure to excel, study, or be the person that everyone wanted him to be.

The next round was another shot, and RJ wasn't even sure what this drink was called. But it was sweet and sugary, and it went down easily.

Kevin went out to the dance floor, and RJ made a move to follow him. But a girl pulled him back to the table by his hand. She was laughing and talking, but RJ really couldn't focus on the words. She was pretty, with blonde hair and blue eyes. Two of her friends were at the table with the two other players from the team. They were all laughing about something, but RJ couldn't quite piece it together.

After some prodding, RJ agreed to do another round of shots with the girls. But when the bartender brought the shots out, the blonde slid the glass between her breasts. RJ thought the drink was for her, but she quickly explained that the object was for him to get the glass out and drink it without using his hands. He stood there, staring at the glass and wondering how he was going to do that. Fortunately, one of the other guys stepped forward and showed him how it was done.

The girl laughed amiably, understanding that he was new to this. RJ thought that perhaps she liked the fact that he hadn't done this 100 times with 100 other girls. For whatever reason, she got another shot and repeated her maneuver. This time, RJ wrapped his lips around the glass and tilted his head back. The alcohol burned on the way down. In surprise, he dropped the glass, which fortunately bounced off his shoe and rolled under the table. One of the other girls picked it up.

Now the girl led him out to the dance floor. RJ felt confined by the small amount of space, but the blonde didn't seem to mind. She moved in closer and danced up against him—swaying her hips against his, and occasionally letting her hand run down his arm or shoulder. RJ knew he should remove himself from this situation, but the booze and pills made it difficult for him to think clearly, much less articulate why he wanted to leave.

When the music slowed to a ballad, RJ felt the girl move much closer to him. She pressed herself against him, and more or less swayed, since that was all that RJ was capable of at the moment. He knew from the look on the blonde's face that she could tell he was aroused.

He looked around for Kevin to help him out, but he didn't spot him anywhere. He wanted to leave. At that point, he wasn't feeling all that well, but the blonde kept grinding up against him. She caught his gaze and smiled at him. But RJ finally managed to stumble off the floor.

He found the table where he'd been, but his friends weren't there. He stumbled outside, inhaling the cool air and trying to clear his mind. It helped a little, but not much. He wasn't sure how he was going to make it home by himself. The blonde came outside to talk to him. "What happened? Are you alright?" she asked.

After a racking heave, RJ unloaded his dinner and shots all over the girl and the ground. She ran off in the other direction, leaving him to do it twice more. He couldn't taste or smell anything except the acidy bile from his stomach. He wished he knew of a place to wash up, but that would involve going home. And he wasn't sure that he could make it all that way without throwing up more. However, without Kevin or the other players, there was no other choice for him but to head home.

So RJ started stumbling in the direction of the dorm, or at least what he hoped was that direction. As he weaved down the sidewalk, he saw flashes of people stepping around him or moving aside to avoid him. Then, when he came to a corner, he couldn't remember which way to turn to go to his dorm. He stood there for a moment—trying to debate which option was best, and not having any luck.

When the light at the corner changed, RJ took a step forward. Then his world turned dark.

When RJ awoke, he wasn't at the dorm or at home. He opened an eye and looked around, but he couldn't make sense of where he was. He knew that he'd gone out for drinks at McCabe's, but the night was fuzzy after that. RJ closed his eyes again and drifted off.

When he awoke again, the sun was shining through the window. He could hear the whisper of soft voices in the next room. Maybe he'd been wrong. Maybe it was his room, and Kevin was trying to get some woman out of there without waking him. RJ opened an eye and saw that it definitely wasn't his room. Then he looked down. These weren't his clothes either.

He winced, truly hoping that he hadn't gone home with that blonde from last night. He'd been tempted to sleep with her. She'd made it clear that she wanted to, but as pissed as he was at Mya, RJ still couldn't cross that line with another woman. He wanted to be a one-woman guy.

Now he was sure that he wasn't in someone's bedroom. He moved his arm, and it wouldn't move the way he wanted it to. Had something happened to him last night? Had he been hit by a car? He shifted his head and saw that an IV ran from his hand up into a bag of fluid. RJ hoped that it was only saline. He tried to remember more of what he'd done, but it was hazy.

He dozed again. When he woke this time, there was a nurse in the room. "How are you feeling?" she asked, standing a few feet from the bed and reading a chart.

"Like crap. What's going on?" RJ used his free hand to wipe his eyes.

"It's not surprising that you don't remember anything. You were pretty far gone when you came in here."

"I'd been drinking."

"You nearly had alcohol poisoning," she corrected. "You'd had way too much to drink, especially given the fact that you're not 21 yet."

"How do you—" RJ started.

"Driver's license and college ID." She made a few notations on the chart, checked the bag of fluid, and left the room.

RJ felt entirely alone. Although it was his own doing, he was sick, and no one was there with him. He didn't want his family to know, but none of his teammates were there. He wasn't sure how he'd gotten there. Had someone transported him? He also wasn't sure how he'd get home.

When the nurse came in again, she checked his blood pressure, his pulse, and his temperature. They must have been okay, because she brought him some crackers, Jell-O, and soda. "Keep these down, and we'll let you go home."

RJ nodded and nibbled at a cracker. It tasted like sand in his mouth, but he kept chewing and swallowed. The scratching sensation went all the way down his throat. He sipped at the soda, which burned like the drinks last night. However, he didn't feel an urge to vomit, so he ate some more. The Jell-O was cool, and seemed to ease the burning in his throat.

When he was finished with the food, he pressed the call button on the bed. Then he explained that he felt like he was ready to leave. A nurse came in, and brought in a bag of clothing and some papers to sign.

The clothes were nasty. He'd obviously thrown up on himself several times. The nurse excused herself and came back with the shirt portion of some scrubs. "Use this. We don't have any jeans or pants, but at least your shirt will be cleaner."

He got dressed and looked at the papers. They were all medical forms and insurance coverage. "Can't I pay cash?"

"Good luck with that. You stayed here overnight. Even if we could get a billing person here on a Sunday morning, the billing would be in the thousands. I doubt you have that much cash on you."

He moaned, realizing that his parents would soon find out about this incident. Not only would they be disappointed, they'd have to pay for it. The only insurance they had was the crappy stuff that Dad got through the school district. So they'd owe hundreds of dollars that they didn't have.

So now he'd made a fool of himself, informed his family about his drinking, and cost them a fortune. RJ wanted to scream, but he didn't want to freak out the nurse. Then she might want to hold him for observation.

He put his shoes on, signed the rest of the forms, and waited. An attendant with a wheelchair rolled him down to the lobby. RJ was debating how to get home, when he saw a familiar face. His English TA was in the lobby, reading a book. "Feeling better?" he asked.

RJ made a face. "Yeah, how did you know about this? Are people talking?"

The TA studied RJ's face for a minute. "Man, you were bad off. I'm the one who picked you up off the concrete and drove you here. It turns out that TAs should not try to pick up football players, even if they are star quarterbacks."

"What? You did this?"

The TA nodded. "Yeah, someone had to."

"Why? I guess you're a football fan?" RJ scowled at him. He'd really thought that a friend had brought him, not a teacher. This guy would probably tell the professor the whole sad story, and they could have a good laugh before they gave him a grade that tanked his scholarships.

"Not quite. I don't know a wide receiver from a television receiver. But you are a student of mine, and one with promise. So I thought I'd intervene."

RJ ran a hand over his face. "Wow, uh, thanks I guess."

"We provide an all-purpose education here."

"Well, thanks again. Why are you still here?" RJ looked around. The lobby was empty, except for a coffee kiosk that was opening.

"Figured you might need a ride home. This place is about three miles from campus. It's a long walk."

They walked out to the TA's car. "My clothes probably stink, though. Do you have a towel or something for me to sit on?"

The TA grabbed something from the trunk and threw it down on the seat. "There. Just lean back, and I'll have you there in a few minutes, okay?"

RJ closed his eyes, but still felt slightly dizzy. So he opened them again. He was glad that he didn't have to try to walk this. He wondered what had happened to Kevin and the other guys from last night. He hoped they were okay.

The car stopped in front of the dorm. "Here you go."

RJ stopped and looked at the TA. "Hey, what's your name? I can't say thanks, if I don't even know who you are."

The TA stuck out his hand. "It's Mark. Go get some sleep, and I'll see you tomorrow."

RJ headed inside the dorm, walked up the flight of stairs, and went into his room. Kevin wasn't there. He wondered where his roommate was. But first, he needed to shower and get out of these clothes. He was surprised to by how hungry he was. So he grabbed a quick shower and headed to breakfast.

RJ saw one of the guys from the bar eating with several people he didn't recognize. The guy gave him a nod, then went back to eating.

As RJ put his tray away, he stopped by the guy's table. "What happened to you all last night?"

The guy looked at his friends and laughed. "Dude, you were so wasted. We were dancing. Then suddenly, you were gone. We figured you went home with some girl. We just stayed there and danced until the place closed. You missed a lot of fun."

RJ thought about the puking, the disorientation, and his time in the hospital. He didn't want to be a part of this lifestyle. He'd thought that Kevin's life wasn't for him since he met him, but now he knew for sure. He walked away from the table without saying a word.

He'd just gotten to the dorm when his cell rang. As he pulled it out of his pocket, he noticed that he'd missed calls from Mya and his grandfather. He'd get to those later.

"Hello?"

"RJ, this is Coach. I need to talk to you now. How soon can you be here?" His voice was stern and crisp. It was not the voice of someone who'd won a game yesterday. It was the voice of someone who was angry.

"Twenty minutes?" RJ said, looking at the time on his phone. "Will that work?"

"Just make it as fast as you can." The line went dead before RJ could ask the Coach what was going on.

In twenty minutes, he was sitting in front of the coach's desk, waiting to hear what was going on. "I want to talk to you about last night."

RJ looked at him. "What about last night?" He hoped that the coach was talking about something other than what happened outside the bar.

The coach slid a piece of paper across the desk. "This."

RJ scanned the paper. It was from the student newspaper at State. There was an article about the football team, underage drinking, and unsportsmanlike behaviors. A photo was on one side of the article. Even in the grainy printout, RJ could see that it was a photo of him—passed out on the sidewalk, much as Mark had described it. Apparently, the person who took this photo saw more of an opportunity to make some money than to help him.

"Do you have anything to say about this?" Coach said. "You can't believe the amount of shit I'm getting about it."

"About a few drinks?" RJ asked.

"It's more than a few drinks. The Athletic Director saw this. He's livid. Apparently, after this photographer saw you last night, they went back to McCabe's and got photos of several of the other members on the team doing shots, making out with women, and behaving inappropriately. All of them are under 21, and all of them are on the football team. The paper is calling for a full investigation of underage drinking at the school, as well as other behaviors."

"Other behaviors?" RJ asked with an uneasy feeling about where this might be heading. He wondered if the ADHD pills that he'd been snorting would show up in a drug test. That would not be good. Drinking might be swept under the rug as youthful indiscretion, but drug use was a major policy violation in the NCAA.

"Drug use. I want you to look me in the eye, and tell me that you could pass a drug test right now—this minute. If I passed you a cup right now, would it come back clean?" Coach met RJ's gaze and didn't blink. He kept his eyes on RJ, who squirmed in his seat. Coach quickly made an assessment. "So it's like that, is it? I really hoped that you'd be different. Damn."

Coach picked up the phone and dialed a number. "Sommers? Yeah, I have Robinson here right now, and he's confirmed that drug use was also involved. I doubt that he could pass a piss test at the moment. I know. I know. Yeah."

He hung up the phone and looked at RJ. "The AD is on his way down. We're going to quash this story in the newspaper, on one condition: that these behaviors stop. You're going to need to keep your nose clean—literally— until you graduate. If we cover this up, you have to guarantee that you'll stop."

The AD knocked on the door and entered. His face was grim. "So what exactly have you gotten yourself into here?"

RJ recounted the entire story: his troubles with keeping up with school assignments, staying awake after he sprained his ankle, and getting invited to go out and party. He didn't leave out any details about what had been going on. He concluded by recounting events from the night before.

When he finished, the AD didn't say a word. RJ cringed, thinking of the shame of having to tell his grandfather about being weak and using drugs. Then he thought about telling Mya and watching her face contort in disappointment. She'd think that their future had been compromised because he had wanted to have a good time—while she worked two jobs, battled with an old car, and tried to get an education. Her reaction would be worse than any sentence meted out by the school.

The AD started talking. "How deep does this go? I'm assuming that you weren't alone at the bar, given the photos and the article."

RJ shrugged. "They were all drinking. I don't know about anything else."

The AD looked at Coach. "Let's talk about this." He looked at RJ and pointed toward the door. "Wait outside until we're done."

Those twenty minutes were among the longest of RJ's life. He was concerned about being kicked off the team and losing his chance at the pros. It was all too much, and because of his stupid actions, his fate was being decided by other men. He didn't like that feeling at all.

Finally, the door opened, and the AD said, "RJ, why don't you come back in?"

The forced politeness of the AD was more than RJ could bear. If he'd been shouting at him, RJ could have handled it better. He'd dealt with shouting before. But this false quietness was more than he could take.

"Let's go over this. First, I'll tell you the upside. We talked to the student newspaper. They've agreed to pull the article from the website and clean their cache—whatever that means. But it's gone. So there are no worries about it going public. I doubt that anyone will see it since it's only been up for a couple hours on a Sunday morning."

RJ beamed. "Thank you so much, sir. I can't tell you how much I appreciate it."

The man scoffed. "You might not say that after you've heard the downside. You'll be doing monthly drug tests until you graduate. There will be no more drinking—period. We're also setting up a study program for you. You'll be expected to report to the library three days a week. You'll be checking in with a tutor there, who will record the hours. I don't expect that you'll need any additional teaching from the tutor, but he'll be making sure that you're using your time wisely."

"That all sounds reasonable to me." RJ was actually relieved to have some structure again. Since the injury, all the hours being alone and not practicing had likely contributed to this debacle.

"Good. Coach will have a document drawn up, which will list all the new rules that you'll be expected to follow. That way, there'll be no confusion about what you're going to be doing."

RJ nodded. "Yes, sir."

The AD left without another word. Coach cleared his throat. "It's your choice about whether or not you share your plan with anyone else on the team. I'll be talking to the team tomorrow at practice about random drug testing. I wasn't aware that these things were going on here this year. I thought I'd put a stop to it."

RJ nodded. "I take full responsibility for this. Nobody made me do these things."

"That's a good attitude, son, but I also know the off-field pressures that can be placed on a player like you. It's a lot to take. I didn't want to say this in front of the AD, but you also need to stop having meals with agents. For all I know, you paid for your own meal, but it looks bad. And right now, everyone in the athletic program is going to be looking at you. Understand?"

RJ nodded. "It won't happen again."

"Then that'll be all." Coach slid the copy of the article over to RJ. "You might want to keep this as a reminder of what could happen. This is the side of professional athletics that most people don't read about. But I would have thought that you—of all people—would know better."

The words stung. RJ could only imagine that Coach was talking about his dreams and goals. He'd been stupid to almost piss everything away over a good time. He wouldn't let that happen again.

RJ took the paper and stuffed it in his pocket. "Yes, sir."

Back at the dorm, the room stunk from RJ's clothes, which hadn't been washed. So he threw the article on his desk and started a load of laundry.

After RJ started a second load of laundry, he looked at the assignments that needed to be completed that week. Then the crumpled paper caught his eye, so he decided to read the article in full—to see exactly what had been discovered about his night out.

As it turned out, most of the article was just speculation. Obviously, RJ wasn't to confirm or deny anything after he passed out. No wonder they agreed to take it down: They suggested drug use without having any proof. They had photos of Kevin and some of the other guys at McCabe's doing body shots off of some girl. But other than that, they didn't even have proof that RJ was at that bar.

RJ read the last paragraph, which puzzled him. "We're disappointed in superstar RJ Robinson. We assumed that he would have learned from his father's time at State."

RJ was stunned. He didn't even know that his father attended State. He must have gone to school somewhere since he was a teacher, but he never talked about specifics. *Is that why he never wants to come here? Because he had a bad time in school? Did something traumatic happen, or did he just miss Mom?* RJ knew that his parents started dating in high school, but he didn't know what happened between them while they were in college. Mom went to Dartmouth, which was a huge expense to her parents. RJ always assumed that Dad also went there, or somewhere nearby.

Now he realized that his parents' relationship was similar to his relationship with Mya. He liked that idea, and it bolstered his sagging ego about their relationship.

So what was RJ supposed to have learned from his father? The tone of the article implied that his father had a reputation for partying in school, but he'd never seen his dad take a drink—ever. Now RJ wondered if the reason was that he's an alcoholic.

Now his curiosity was overwhelming him. What did Coach say? Something about how he—of all people—should have known better? At first, RJ assumed that this statement had something to do with being a star quarterback or being diligent, but now he thought that it might have something to do with his dad. If he had a reputation at state for heavy drinking, that would explain why Coach expected RJ to know better.

RJ logged onto his computer. He googled Robert Robinson, but all he found were articles about himself. There were pages and pages. When he tried to add keywords like "State" to the search, it didn't help. The articles were all about recent games, and RJ's performance on the field.

So RJ decided to try to add some phrases that would only apply to his father. He did some quick calculations, and came up with the years that his father attended college.

When he put in the years, the number of hits drastically dropped. The first few pages were still about RJ, but on pages 4 and 5, there were articles about other people. But he still had to wade through articles about a biologist and a preacher before getting to the ones about his father.

RJ sat there in stunned silence. The comments suddenly made sense: His father played football at State.

He didn't understand how he hadn't known. How could he be 19-years-old, and only now discover this information by googling it? Didn't anyone think to mention that his father had also been a quarterback 20 years earlier?

He read two articles about games that his father quarterbacked. Both of them ended with State winning by double digits. His scores were fantastic, and RJ would kill to have those stats. Even with his own running records, he doubted that he could ever beat the records his father set here. Why didn't anyone ever mention these games?

RJ would love to try to beat his father's stats. Wouldn't that competition bring them closer together? Maybe his dad didn't want to be close to RJ. He never went to any of his games. He always had an excuse. Was it because he knew that RJ would never be the player that he was? That would be a pretty harsh statement to make about a kid in elementary school.

RJ still couldn't get the notion through his head. He kept scrolling through pages and pages of search results. In a few cases, he found articles about games his father had won, records he'd set, and bowl games he'd played in. There were probably more stories in the archives somewhere, but since the internet was newer back then, all of his father's games probably weren't listed in the results.

RJ was able to piece together parts of his father's first two years at State. Apparently, he took the team to the Rose Bowl at the end of his sophomore season. There was speculation that he might skip his last two years of school to go to the pros. Then the articles stopped.

RJ skimmed through another 50 pages of search results, but he couldn't find any mention of his father after that. It was as though he'd dropped off the face of the earth. Except he hadn't. RJ knew right where he was. He was destined to be this phenomenal football star. But now he was a high school PE teacher, who didn't even coach football or bother to go to his son's games.

There was only one way to find out what happened: ask his father directly. It would be the first real conversation they'd had in ages.

Chapter 13

KEVIN STILL WASN'T in the dorm when RJ started looking for a ride home. So he found another teammate who was willing to loan him his car. RJ didn't think that he'd ever need to hurry home, but now he did. The car was a newer black Buick, decked out with all the luxuries. He wondered if it belonged to his teammate's parents, or if he'd gotten it as a payoff from an agent. RJ knew that he was taking a risk by borrowing the car if it had been improperly given, but he wanted to go home. Now that he knew about his father's football career, he wanted an explanation as soon as possible.

RJ decided not to call Mya before he left. She probably would have talked him out of it. Her family was big on keeping the peace, which is the last thing RJ wanted at that moment.

The two-hour trip flew by. It should have: The ride had Sirius radio, cruise control, and heated seats. RJ practiced what he was going to say to his father over and over, until he'd almost memorized it. He was still angry about the newfound knowledge. His father skipped all of RJ's games and practices—without so much as a word of explanation. All those missed opportunities to be closer to his dad. All those years that his grandfather neglected to mention that his son had done the same things as his grandson before he was born. It felt like a giant conspiracy had been perpetrated: A scheme to keep him in the dark about his own family.

He pulled into the driveway of his parents' house and stopped the car. He took a deep breath and marched inside.

His mother looked up from her laptop. "RJ, what are you doing home? We weren't expecting you."

"I bet you weren't," RJ replied. His father was dozing in an recliner by the television, which was showing a repeat of a BBC comedy on the local PBS station.

RJ marched over to the television, picked up the remote, and changed the station to an NFL game. The Cardinals were playing the Seahawks. His mother just gaped at him, but his father sat up and said, "What do you think you're doing? I don't want to watch that." His eyes were bright, and his face reddened.

"Bring back too many memories, Dad?" RJ spat out the words like they were pebbles.

"What are you talking about? I was just watching something else on TV." He reached for the remote control, but RJ snatched it away. He was going to get to the bottom of this, and he thought that a football game was an appropriate soundtrack for this conversation.

"I thought I'd come home. We can talk about football, and you can tell me about your experiences at State. A little bonding time."

RJ's father didn't say a word. He silently sat in his chair, eyeing the remote. However, RJ's mother stood up and walked over to her son.

"Is that what this is about? You learned about your father, and you're angry?" She tried to put her arm around RJ, but he shook her hand away.

"Hell yes, I'm angry. People keep referring to it, and I have no idea what they're talking about. I have to google it to find out something that everyone else already knows. You didn't really think that I was going to make it through four years at the same school without a single person mentioning this to me, did you?" RJ stood there, swiveling his head back and forth between his parents. His mother looked like she wanted to comfort him, but didn't know how. His father just sat there, still not moving or talking.

"RJ, if we'd known you'd hear something, I would have told you myself. I can tell you about it now if you'd like."

His mother's voice was calm and soothing, and he had a hard time staying angry, especially since he needed comfort at that moment.

But RJ didn't want to just give in and sweep everything under the rug again. He always knew that something was wrong with his family. His father's response was too apathetic, too uncaring. It wasn't normal. But RJ could never put his finger on why before. He just accepted it as reality.

His parents were waiting for him to reply. Did he want to know this story? Did he really want to find out what made them turn out this way? His father was on the cusp of a professional football career with his entire future ahead of him, and now he sat in a recliner in a small town in Connecticut. How fast and how far must he have fallen to get there?

"I'd like to hear it from Dad. It's his story." RJ turned and faced his father.

The man got up from his chair and left the room. RJ thought of going after him, but what then? You can't make an adult do something they don't want to do. He wished that his dad was supportive, but he was more like a shadow than a father. And this discovery apparently wasn't going to change that. Knowledge or not, RJ would never bond with his dad over his college days.

He turned to his mother. "I guess I don't have a choice. I'll have to hear it from you." The words oozed with resentment. RJ didn't remember ever being this angry before. Even at this point, his father wouldn't come through for him. He'd rather abandon him than talk about it.

"Well, your grandfather always loved football," she started. Her face was a mix of emotions. RJ could see the anxiety and concern, but other emotions roiled under the surface, which he couldn't identify. He wondered what was going on in his mother's mind at that moment.

"I already knew that," RJ huffed, sitting in the now-vacant recliner. At least then his father couldn't sit there while she told the story. If he wasn't going to tell it, then RJ really didn't want him to be there to hear it.

"You weren't his first project. Your father was," she continued.

RJ thought about that statement, and it made sense. If his grandfather was so keen on the sport, then he'd definitely try to get his only son interested in it. He hadn't skipped a generation.

"Your father never cared for football, not like you do. He did it mainly to please his dad. He started out when he was five. That's one reason why we were adamant that you weren't going to start that early. It was too soon. Your father had practice once a week, and games on Saturday.

It was pretty grueling for a kid who didn't even have all of his adult teeth yet."

"But he was good, right?" RJ asked, thinking about what he'd read in those online articles. They didn't sound like stories about someone who didn't like football. They sounded like stories about a star.

"He was very good. That was the problem. He was very good, but unmotivated." His mother looked off into the distance, as if she was remembering him from those days.

"So what happened?"

His mom shrugged. "The same thing that happens every time a parent wants something that their child doesn't. The parent wins, and the child does what the parent wants."

"So he kept playing? That's how he got so good?"

His mother turned to face him. Her eyes were welling up, but she didn't cry. RJ felt bad for pushing her to this point, but he needed to know what happened. "Your grandfather was insistent. You know how he can be. Everything he did with you, he did with your father. He used the exact same pattern. It was upsetting, especially to your father."

RJ stared at her. "Yet you never said anything. Why not? If it was so upsetting, why didn't you say anything to me about it?"

His mother dabbed at her eyes. "Trust me, we said something. We talked with your grandfather about it until we were blue in the face. But it didn't matter. Despite our complaints, he drafted you. He made sure you wanted to do play football more than anything. If you were enjoying it, what were we supposed to say?"

RJ felt his face flush. Had he really been manipulated that easily? "You could have talked to me about this. You could have told me Dad's story, and that you didn't approve."

His mother sighed. "I would have had to do it alone. When your grandfather drafted you, you loved it. But your father wouldn't have anything to do with a discussion about football. You saw him today. He wasn't any better in those days than he is now."

"So you just let me go on? Why wouldn't you tell me what happened to Dad?"

His mom's eyes started welling up again. "Because it's his story. I always thought that when the time was right, he'd step up and tell you. But I guess not."

RJ felt tears sting his eyes, too. It had been one hell of a day. From his near-expulsion to the revelation about his family's past to his father's refusal to explain it, he felt alienated from everyone he knew. "I guess not. Apparently he told you all about it, though. So I guess he just doesn't like me."

"Don't kid yourself," his mother said, her tone getting sharp. "I only know about these things because I was there and saw it all. We've dated since our freshman year of high school. No one had to tell me anything."

His mother's tone was surprising. There was a tinge of bitterness that he hadn't heard before. Perhaps he wasn't the only one who was frustrated with his dad's lack of communication skills.

"Anyway, your father kept playing throughout middle school and high school. The team was undefeated during their senior year. Even though he didn't particularly like playing, it was part of his identity by then. He'd always done it. And after all that time playing, he thought of himself as a football player. That was who he was: a jock."

"So how did you two meet?" RJ asked, thinking about Mya. He still felt betrayed by how she'd left so suddenly with someone else that weekend.

"The normal way. A friend of mine knew your father because they lived in the same neighborhood. She introduced us at a party, and we started dating. Underneath the jock exterior, I could see there was a guy who didn't really like playing sports. He liked to read and think about things. He was sensitive and kind and a million things that you wouldn't have thought a football player would be." His mother smiled at the thought. "We started dating, as the season allowed. Your grandfather was strict about when we could see each other, and how often we could go out."

RJ was puzzled for a moment. "Interesting, because Grandpa was one of the ones who really encouraged me to date Mya. But you and Dad didn't seem like you wanted me to see her. Why?"

"Your dad didn't want you to end up like him. He thought that any change he made in your life might affect the outcome. He liked Mya, but he didn't want you to end up like him."

"Because of Grandpa?"

"Yeah, sometimes I think that your grandfather believes that he made a mistake about being so strict about us—because then your father would have dumped me, and kept his football career."

RJ couldn't see how those two things could be related. It didn't seem like Mya had much to do with his recent, bad decision-making. He was responsible for the mess he was in. He thought about just leaving and going to see her, but at the moment, he was still smarting from their last encounter. Soon, but not yet.

"We saw each other at school all the time. I was with him when he got the word that State offered him a full ride. We were thrilled. But I didn't want to go to State, because I needed a school with a better writing program. We were close enough to visit and talk all the time—even before they had smartphones."

RJ tried to imagine his parents as young and in love, but it was hard. His father had never shown any happiness about his life or his fate. Was he miserable about *everything* that happened to him? "So I still haven't heard what happened to Dad. What's so bad that he wouldn't tell his own son about it, even when I found out I was going to State?"

RJ knew that when he had kids, he'd guide them through life. And he'd happily support them, whether or not they wanted to play sports.

"Patience, sweetie. I'll get to it. Let me tell this story in my own way." She gave him a smile and patted his hand. "It just kept getting worse. I knew something was wrong, but he wouldn't really talk about it. The situation got to the point that he wouldn't return my calls, and I was supposed to be his fiancée. He'd be out partying all day and night with the team. Your dad had this wad of cash, and he used it to pay for his friends to party with him. He was doing all sorts of things. It was ugly." His mom looked like she might cry for a second. Her eyes grew moist, and she sniffed. RJ waited for her to blow her nose and continue.

"I really thought that it was his plan for breaking up with me. I figured that he'd had a taste of the good life, and decided that he could do better. He was in his junior year, and there was a lot of pressure about what teams to try out for. Scouts from the teams came to visit him, and offered him ridiculous amounts of money. So much money that we couldn't even imagine it. Then one night, he showed up unannounced at my dorm. He'd been crying. I figured he was going to tell me he'd met someone else."

RJ wondered if that's where his relationship with Mya was going. He assumed that the distance he felt between them lately was on her part. She'd developed a whole new set of friends at school, but what if the distance was on him? Was he pulling away when things got tough? He resolved to think about that more once he'd gotten these things taken care of.

"So what happened then? Obviously, you didn't break up, at least not for good."

"He came to tell me that he was leaving football. He had a huge fight with his father about it. Then the coach came down on him hard, yelling at him for all the stupid mistakes he'd made. Apparently, your father had gotten busted taking cash and gifts from the boosters, and he'd failed a drug test. They ran a full scan after the first test, and they found even more drugs the second time around. He was in grave danger of being suspended, possibly expelled. So he just quit."

"Why did he quit? He was so close to all that money—to that dream."

A voice from behind him said, "Apparently, you haven't been listening. I didn't like football that much. It was just a means to an end. I love your mother, and I like sports. The concentration on football all came from your grandfather."

"So what happened?" RJ said, struggling to believe that he was actually talking to his father about something important.

"Nothing. I quit. I had to pay for my last year of college at a local school. They didn't have an easy area of study, the way State did. So I went with PE as a major. It wasn't as much fun, but at least it was something."

"But what happened with the team at school?" RJ was incredulous that his father made the decision seem so easy, so simple. How could it be that simple to give up such a lucrative dream? The money was too tempting to just give it all up.

"Nothing happened. They said goodbye to me, and I left. The team missed me for a bit. Then they got involved with the whole NFL thing during their senior year, so they forgot all about me."

RJ knew that he couldn't imagine any of his teammates being his friends in ten years. Kevin would be a memory.

"Don't you miss it?" RJ had gotten used to the adulation and praise. He liked the attention, and to be honest, he liked the lifestyle that could go with it. He liked the nice cars and good meals. He didn't know what he'd do if he had to leave football completely. He'd be lost.

"Son, when I look back on my choices, leaving football was probably the best one I ever made." His father smiled, which was rare. In fact, RJ couldn't remember how long it had been since he'd actually seen him smile. Months? Maybe even years?

"What brought all this on? Why were you looking me up?" His father's eyes grew wary as he looked at his son. Just like that, the bonding was over. RJ hadn't thought of a good answer to that question. How was he going to explain his own predicament?

"Uh... Coach mentioned something about me being like you. I wanted to know what he meant, so I looked you up," RJ said, trying to stick as close to the truth as possible.

"How is old Mosby?" his father asked.

RJ was stunned. He knew that Coach had been there a long time, but even with all his research, he never realized that they actually shared the same coach at State. Coach had been there for over 25 years, so the timing was definitely right. It made RJ feel like more of a clone, and less of his own person. He couldn't have followed more in his father's footsteps if he'd been given a map. Why didn't Coach say anything about it to him before? Did he just assume that RJ knew everything, and shared his father's feeling that he shouldn't talk about it?

Or was Coach in some way ashamed of the situation? After all, RJ's dad was nearly expelled. In either case, RJ couldn't understand why nothing was ever said. At least a word in passing would have been appropriate. Why was there this shroud of secrecy surrounding the whole thing? RJ wondered why he wasn't told about any of this.

RJ figured that he wouldn't learn that now—if ever. He could see his dad chafing at the thought of sharing any more feelings or experiences.

RJ looked at his watch. It was getting late, and he had an early class the next morning. "I should get going," he said. He still had tons of questions, but he knew that some of them could be answered by Coach. And perhaps he could just come to an understanding about other ones on his own.

"Why don't you stay tonight? You can get up early. I'll cook you breakfast, and you can head back in time for your class. It would be nice to have you here. I've missed having you around." His mom smiled at him. The tears were gone, and things had returned to normal already. Could RJ let things go just like that? He didn't know, but he suspected that he couldn't. This revelation was too big to just forget in a few minutes.

However, the thought of sleeping in his own bed appealed to him. He needed a sense of security at that moment. He wasn't going to call Mya and let her know that he was home. She was probably out with her friends—or maybe that other guy. He bristled again, just thinking of him riding alone for four hours with her, talking and laughing. He missed all the time he spent with her, but he wasn't going to say anything now. He'd wait until he had this family stuff straightened out.

"You know that would mean making me breakfast at five?" RJ asked, thinking about how he used to get up that early every morning without a problem. Now the idea made his head hurt. It seemed like the middle of the night. He thought about how spoiled and undisciplined he'd become over the past four months. He pondered the idea of getting back into that routine, just to get away from the easy side of life.

"Yeah, I know. I've done it before, and I'm sure it won't be my last time." She sighed and stood up. RJ looked around and realized that his father had left the room without a word. That was typical. "You'd better hit the sack. You don't want to be tired for English tomorrow."

RJ raised an eyebrow at her. She knew his schedule.

"Of course I know when my favorite class is being held. I don't know your practice schedule, but I know that." She laughed. "Now get to bed."

RJ opened the door to his room. It felt like the last time he had slept there was a lifetime ago. But in reality, it had only been a few months. He noticed that the room was swept and dusted. And while some of his mess had been neatly stacked into piles, the overall feel of the room hadn't changed much. He was glad to be back in familiar surroundings. It felt good.

He quickly stripped, and didn't even bother to brush his teeth. He just slid under the covers, and immediately fell asleep.

Chapter 14

THE NEXT MORNING, RJ made it back to class with plenty of time to spare. He dropped a few things back at his dorm, where there still weren't any signs of Kevin. He returned the car key to his teammate and headed for class. The discussion from last night still weighed heavily on his mind, and his mind drifted off more than once.

At one point, Mark the TA approached him and asked, "Are you doing okay? You seem a million miles away."

RJ cleared his throat. "I'll tell you after class, if that's okay?" He surprised himself with that question. He wasn't planning on talking to anyone about this, but the words just slipped out. It wasn't like he could damage the TA's viewpoint of him any further. After all, Mark saw him throw up and pass out on a street corner. After that spectacle, family drama would seem insignificant.

Mark nodded and went back to teaching. By the end of class, RJ had repeatedly thought about making a dash out the door, but that would only buy him until Wednesday, when he'd see Mark again.

"So what's up?" Mark asked, tidying up a stack of papers. RJ wondered how much time Mark spent grading papers. He knew that Mark didn't put in the same number of hours that he spent practicing football, but it was probably close.

Briefly, RJ relayed everything he'd learned about his father's football career.

"Literature is full of stories about characters following in their fathers' footsteps. Think of Oedipus." Mark laughed at his own joke.

RJ just raised an eyebrow. "That's just nasty. I'm apparently good at the same sport that my dad was. Not a big surprise. I do think athletic ability is genetic—including all the hand-eye coordination, and the ability to think on your feet. That sort of thing. But does that heritage mean that I should make the same mistakes he did?"

"I don't think making the same mistakes is genetic. In this case, I think they're the results of the rewards system we have in place for exceptional athletes. This sort of thing is endemic in sports. The baser emotions that paid sports bring out is just an ugly appeal to the human desire for instant gratification and greed. Everyone suffers from them." Mark shrugged. "If you put people in a particularly stressful situation, most of them are going to act out."

"So what would you do?" The words came out, without RJ thinking about them. He was surprised that he was asking someone he barely knew to give him advice. But he was doubting his trust in Mya and his family. And Coach had known about his father all along, and said nothing. Until that moment, RJ didn't realize how absolutely alone he felt.

Mark's eyes grew wide. "Wow, no idea. I've never been in that situation. I do know that if something made me unhappy—and I didn't see that situation changing—then I'd try to find something else to do. But if I had a chance at a Pulitzer after four years of stress, it would be challenging not to want to deal with the stress."

"So the short version is that you don't know?"

Mark shrugged. "Pretty much. I'm not you. I don't have the same pressures that you do. I'm working on a graduate degree in English. The prospect of seven digits doesn't even enter my vocabulary. So it's hard to see myself in your shoes. Go with what makes you happy. Life is too short to be miserable."

RJ slumped over a bit in his seat. "I thought Mya made me happy, but I'm not sure now. She got a ride down here with some guy, and they seemed like they were having way too much fun. So I think I may have lost her."

Mark cleared his throat. "Mr. Robinson, you need to read more of the classics. *Much Ado about Nothing* would be a good choice for you right now. You're making all sorts of assumptions about your girlfriend—without any facts to back them up. You need to just call her and talk about it. If people just addressed what was going on with them, most works of fiction would be finished within 20 pages."

RJ nodded. "I've been wanting to, but I'm afraid of what I'll hear."

"In your mind, she's already walking out the door. What could be worse than that? You need to call her."

RJ gave him a small smile. "Thanks. I will. I really appreciate the talk."

Mark took a deep bow from the waist. "I'm an all-purpose assistant. I can help with both scholastic and personal issues." He gave RJ a smile, and threw his backpack over his shoulder. "Good luck with everything."

RJ had some time before his next class, so he texted Mya and asked her about talking. She responded in seconds, and before he could finish typing a response, his phone rang.

"What's up? Midday call? Must be something important." She didn't sound any different. RJ imagined that she'd be cold and distant, paving the way for a breakup.

RJ told her everything that had happened since the game. With each retelling, it felt more real—and less like a fantasy that was happening to someone else. It also took some of the sting out of it, which made everything seem more manageable. If he could accept things and move on, then he could think about his future.

"Damn, you've been busy. What's all this about?"

RJ started with the term paper, and told her how impossible it seemed to do what was right and keep up with his school work. Mya asked a few questions, but mostly, she just let him talk.

"So what do you think I should do?" RJ asked when he was finished.

"Is there really something to do here? You've been telling me all this stuff, but it's all in the past. It's done. You learned a lesson. You got spanked for doing something wrong, and I know you well enough to know that you won't do it again. You found out some stuff about your dad, but so what? You're not him. For starters, you called to tell me all this. I don't think your dad calls your mom just to talk."

RJ had to agree. It was good to talk to her about it. Since she knew his family, he didn't have to explain the entire situation. "So just keep on keeping on?"

"Why not? Are you wanting to quit because your dad quit twenty years ago? If everyone was afraid of following in their parent's footsteps, tons of family businesses would go under. There's nothing wrong with doing the same thing that your family did. You just need to do it better."

"Yeah, but I guess I'm just feeling manipulated. I thought my grandfather was encouraging me in a sport that I liked. Now I'm wondering if I ever really liked football, or if he pushed it on me. It didn't matter what kind of kid I was; he would have done the same thing no matter what."

"Well, from what you're telling me, your dad didn't like sports in that way. So he was pushed into something that he didn't love. But you've always loved football. When we met in the stands, you wouldn't stop talking about it. I sometimes wonder if you'd ever have liked me if I didn't love sports so much." She laughed, but RJ could hear a question underneath it.

"Of course I would've. You were the only girl in the stands. I didn't have much of a choice." He wasn't going to make it that easy on her. If she was fishing for a compliment, he'd make her bring out a bigger pole to hook something.

"Thanks. Always the ego builder. So what do you think you're going to do?"

"I don't know. I don't enjoy feeling like I got played, especially when it's something this important. And I don't understand why my parents didn't stand up for me."

"Yeah, well, you have some decisions to make. I'll support you no matter what. You know that, right?"

Her words made him feel comfortable and wanted, as if the situation with Mike had never happened. He wanted to forget about that game. Actually, he wished he could go back in time to that Saturday and do everything differently. "You sure you'll be around?"

There was a long pause on the other end of the phone. RJ's heart raced, and he could feel sweat run down the back of his neck, even though it was November. Was this the end? Was she going to tell him it was over? "Yeah. Why?"

"Well, on Saturday—"

RJ didn't even get to finish his sentence. Mya hooted into the phone. He could hear her laughter, and his face turned red. He hadn't blushed around her in ages, but now, he could feel the flush run up his neck into his face. "You're jealous? Of Mike? Really? RJ Robinson, you should know better by now. Nothing's happening there. Never has been, and never will be."

RJ felt a bit annoyed that she'd cut him off without even considering his point of view. "Yeah, well, it's possible. I mean, you're both good-looking. So why couldn't it happen?"

Mya took a deep breath. "You should already know why by now: I love you. I've loved you for a long time. I loved you before you had a chance at big money in the NFL. I loved you when you were just you, not some sports star. There's never been anyone else, and you should know that. Just like I know you'd never cheat on me."

RJ nodded. Even when he was trashed, he knew that he couldn't cheat on her. She was the only one for him. "Yeah, okay. I know that. It's good to hear it, though. It just seems like it's been too long since we had any time together. We get one night every few weeks. It's tough not to think that you're getting tired with this arrangement."

She snorted. "I won't lie. It's not always easy, but Mike is no problem at all. One of the reasons we bonded in class is because we're the only two minorities in our class. So we can complain about all the privilege in that room."

RJ tried to remember the guy. He had pale skin and was tall with a light brown buzz-cut and large brown eyes. He tried to think of what minority Mike would be, but nothing came to mind. He certainly wasn't Hispanic or African American.

"I think I'm missing something. What is Mike's race?"

His girlfriend sighed deeply. "All minority statuses aren't due to race. What about a sexual minority?"

RJ abruptly stopped walking, which almost caused the girl walking behind him to drop one of her bags. "He's gay?"

"Pretty much. So if anyone has to worry about losing someone to Mike, I should be worried. He thought you were adorable." She laughed again. "I wasn't going to tell you that, but since you're all worried, I'm not going to spare your feelings about it."

"What? But he knew all those stats. He likes football," RJ said and moved to a different area before he was run over by pedestrian traffic. "What's up with that?"

"Two words: Michael Sam. Gay guys can like football, too. Geez, you need to modernize your attitude." RJ could envision Mya right now—standing in a way that exhibited the attitude she was giving him.

"So we're good?"

"Yeah, we're good. But fair warning, I'm going to tell Michael that you were worried. He's going to love that."

RJ rolled his eyes. "Yeah, whatever. I have to go to class."

They said their goodbyes, and RJ made his way across campus to his next class. Without the crutches, it was a much more pleasant walk. He practically sprinted to make it on time. While he hadn't settled anything with

Mya about their future, it felt good to have her back on his side.

He still wasn't sure what to do, but he had time. It wasn't like there was a clock counting down, forcing him to make a decision. He had three more years if he needed them.

RJ had a few more assignments to complete before finals, so he went to the library after dinner. After relaying the events from the past 24 hours multiple times, he was actually glad to be alone.

When Kevin wasn't at the dorm after RJ returned from the library, he wondered if he should be worried about him. The last time he'd seen him was at the bar on Saturday night. For all RJ knew, Kevin could be in a hospital somewhere, suffering from the same issues he'd had.

Kevin had disappeared before, but RJ didn't care about him then. At that time, Kevin was just this annoying guy who occasionally wanted to kick him out of the room. Now they were friends of sorts, even though their relationship would have to change now that RJ was required to stay sober. He would definitely have to cut back on their time together. So RJ decided not to call him yet.

RJ knew that he was ultimately responsible for his own choices, but Kevin had tempted him so many times, like a little devil that sat on his shoulder. Maybe some time away from him would help him readjust his priorities.

When Kevin still didn't show up the next morning, RJ decided to mention it to Coach at practice. But Kevin showed up about two minutes late, acting like nothing had happened.

"Hey, where have you been?" RJ asked, sidling up to him as they walked onto the field. "I haven't seen you since Saturday."

Kevin nodded, sporting a huge grin that spread across his entire face. "You wouldn't believe me if I told you."

RJ rolled his eyes. He already knew where this was going. "You're going to tell me you've spent the past three days having sex? That's it?"

Kevin stopped and turned to face him. "It wasn't just sex. I think I'm falling in love here, RJ. I met this girl at the bar after you left. We danced and went home together. We had sex like you wouldn't believe—for hours! I slept over. Then we woke up and did it again. She went down to the dining hall and brought us back some food. And we did it again after breakfast, and twice more after we ordered pizza for lunch. I swear I thought my dick was going to fall off."

"Okay, that was Sunday. What about since then?" RJ really didn't want to hear about Kevin's sexual exploits. He'd seen and heard more about Kevin's sexual exploits than anyone should have to see or hear. He worried that it would be a bad influence on him, and lead to more pill-popping or another night out on the town.

"After about the seventh or eighth time, we were too worn out for more. So we started talking, and we really hit it off." Kevin made this statement like it was a surprise to him. RJ was rather surprised himself. Falling for a girl would never have been on RJ's List of the Top 20 Things that Kevin Was Doing While MIA for Three Days.

"So you had sex for nearly 24 hours, then talked for 48 hours. You don't do anything halfway, do you?"

Kevin smiled. "Nope. She's coming over to the dining hall tonight. You have to meet her. She's so fine, and you'll like her. Promise."

RJ smirked. "You want me to meet your new girlfriend? Maybe when Mya comes down, we can go on a double date, too."

Kevin nodded enthusiastically. Apparently, RJ's sarcasm didn't register. "Really? You'd do that? That would be great. I don't have many friends who are dating anyone, so it's going to be hard for us to find other couples to hang out with."

RJ just shook his head. He couldn't wrap his mind around all of the things that were happening, and Kevin's transformation was yet another one. He wished there was a way to slow these changes down, and give himself time to process them. But Coach soon had them running and passing the ball.

After practice, Kevin and RJ set a time to eat dinner, so he could meet the new girl. RJ was still weirded out by his roommate's behavior. He'd never seen such a transformation, so he wondered if it would stick. In six months, would Kevin want to go back to his old life of drinking and sleeping with a different girl every night? Was this girl interested in Kevin or the money? What would happen if he got drafted into the NFL after a few months?

When RJ emerged, Coach was standing by the locker-room door. "Hey, can we talk for a minute?" the older man asked.

"Sure, what's up?"

"I got a shock this morning," Coach said, squarely looking RJ in the eye.

"What?" RJ panicked, thinking of their last talk, and the plan that had been imposed on him. What could he have done that would have been reported already?

"Your dad called me." Coach said. Was it his imagination, or did Coach look like he was pitying him? Did he feel sorry for the kid whose dad neglected him and never gave him any life lessons?

RJ just stared. He still had trouble thinking of his father as a young man playing ball for Coach. It was an image that he couldn't envision, no matter how hard he tried. His dad had always just been a dad, not a kid with problems.

"I can see that you're shocked as well. We had a long talk about you."

RJ swallowed hard. He didn't share any of his recent problems with his parents when he went home. That trip had a sole purpose: finding out about his father. He thought the discussion about his own bad behaviors could wait for another day. Now he could see that it wouldn't.

"You didn't tell your parents anything about our talk on Sunday, did you?" RJ felt like Coach was staring right into his soul. He already knew the answer to his own question.

"No, sir. We had other things to talk about."

Coach nodded. "I got a talking-to about the fact that I let it slip that he played for me. Your dad was none-too-happy about that. I forgot what a temper he could have."

RJ tried to incorporate this new knowledge into his head. His father got mad? He hadn't ever seen the man explode. He'd raised his voice once or twice, but that was it. Now Coach was telling him that his dad was angry, and had actually yelled.

"What did he want?" RJ asked. He didn't get much out of his father at home, yet he'd call and berate Coach? This week was getting weirder by the minute.

Coach cleared his throat. "Your dad also called me after you accepted the scholarship to State. He told me that you'd been raised to make your own choices, and that he didn't want you to be influenced by all the choices he'd made. So he made it quite clear to me—and to the whole coaching staff here—that you were not to be told about his time at State."

"Oh," RJ said meekly. So everyone didn't assume that he already knew. Rather, his father deliberately wanted to keep RJ from learning more about him.

"So when I slipped and said something to you on Sunday, you apparently went home to confront him. That's why I got a phone call." Coach's face displayed his displeasure about the call.

RJ shrugged. "Sorry about that. I'd never heard a word of his story until that day. After your comment, I went back to my room and googled it. I had no idea about any of this, so it just blew me away."

Coach nodded. "I understand. Maybe now you more fully understand why I came down on you about the drugs. I don't want you to follow the same path as your father."

RJ's eyes grew wide. "Wait, what? So that's why he quit?"

Coach made a face and groaned loudly. "Shit. I need to just shut my mouth entirely."

"I need to know what really happened."

"Look, RJ. You can't tell your father what I'm telling you. He'd hit the roof. But yeah, your father was doing hardcore drugs. We didn't have a warning about it, the way we did with you. There was a random drug test on the day of the bowl game, and your father didn't pass it. Then they ran a second test, because he was so convincing about being clean. The results were devastating. The bowl game was over, and your father was suspended from the NCAA for a year." Coach looked regretful and sad. RJ thought for a second that Coach might actually lose it and start crying, but he didn't.

"What types of drugs did he use?"

Coach's eyes grew wide. "Why? You want to know how he got caught?"

RJ shook his head. "No, not like that. I just thought they were PEDs, but you sound like you're talking about street drugs."

Coach took a deep breath. "Both, actually. Man, you're going to get me in such trouble." He paused. "After he missed a few practices because of his other problems, he opted to try some steroids and other things to help performance. The pressure that his father put on him was intense."

"Tell me about it," RJ said. "I probably got the exact same set of lectures that my dad did."

"The other drugs were recreational. He probably wouldn't have gotten a suspension for just for them. Nothing was hardcore. So we could have handled that internally. But the PEDs brought him down."

RJ nodded. No wonder his dad left the room when RJ wanted to know more about why he'd quit football. He didn't quit at all; he was forced out for breaking the rules.

He wondered what his grandfather said when he found out. RJ could just imagine the accusations and yelling in that house. At least a large part of his father's history was making sense now. After getting kicked off the team, he returned to his hometown to go to a local college. And after he got his degree, he married Mom. He didn't participate in football, coach it, or even attend games. He totally wrote it out of his life.

RJ wondered if he could do the same. Could he just walk away from all of it and be happy? He truly doubted it. Football was such a part of him. Even if he was banned from the NCAA for life, he'd still want to be a part of it somehow. Whether he naturally loved the game or had merely been indoctrinated, he didn't want to live without it.

Coach watched him as he stood there thinking, but RJ didn't hurry his thoughts. He felt comfortable with who he was, even if he didn't know how he'd arrived at that point.

"So are we good?" Coach asked. "Please don't go running home again, and tell your dad that I've been telling more stories. I can only stand so many phone calls like that."

"Yes, sir." RJ headed back to his dorm. Finals were still a few weeks away. No papers or exams were in the immediate future. Now that he was on a strict program with the athletic department, he'd have to walk the straight and narrow all the time, no matter what was happening.

Kevin had apparently returned, showered, and gone out again. He'd mentioned having dinner with RJ, but was nowhere to be found now. However, RJ knew that he wouldn't be at the bars tonight.

RJ grabbed a quick bite at the dining hall and went to the library to study for a while. He wanted to maintain the time he spent at the library, even if the tutor wasn't there. Tonight, he just read part of *Barchester Towers* for his English class. It wasn't due until Friday, but RJ knew that the game against Sunny Cal State that weekend was important, since the bowl teams would soon be announced. State was expected to easily win the game, but RJ knew that he couldn't take any win for granted.

He kept losing his place in the novel and thinking about his dad. He'd come so close to following the same self-destructive path as his father. While Coach said that recreational drugs could be handled at the university level, RJ knew that the word could get out. He'd have to battle a bad reputation before he even got to the draft. He might be competing against players who didn't have the baggage he had.

RJ thought about Coach's actions. Had he been waiting to see if RJ would make the same mistakes his father made? Addiction could be hereditary, so was RJ just another statistic?

The week went by fast. RJ spent more time at the library studying with the tutor. He didn't get home until later that night, but Kevin never showed up. RJ felt blessed that his roommate wouldn't be able to tempt him with drugs and other pleasures. He wondered how Kevin's new girlfriend would react to stories about his exploits with other women. Would she be jealous of everyone that had come before, or would she feel good that he'd given it all up for her?

The game against Sunny Cal State started slow. Perhaps State had become overconfident, or perhaps Sunny Cal State had improved. Either way, the first half of the game passed without a score.

By the time RJ made it to the locker room, Coach was furiously yelling at the team. "What the hell is going on? What happened to the team that's been winning all year? You look like you all went on vacation and never came back. If you keep this up, you will be on vacation, while the other teams go to the bowl games."

RJ nodded. He knew how much rode on this game. Even with the rough patches he'd experienced, he was still thinking about what the agents had told him. A good season, a bowl game, and the NFL. His sights were still set on all of it.

He and Mya discussed going pro after their freshman year, and she agreed that it was for the best. She was stressed from being poor, which added to the stress that the team placed on him. She wasn't sure that RJ could handle everything for four years without relapsing.

"What about you, Robinson? Stop trying to run the ball. Sunny Cal State gives up goals by passing. I know that, and you should too. I want to see more passing in the second half." Coach's voice was loud and embarrassing. RJ couldn't remember the last time he'd been called out for not giving his all to a game. He felt his face flush. The entire team knew that Coach thought he wasn't doing his best.

RJ wondered if his performance had anything to do with the phone call from his dad. Had Coach been so pissed about the call that he was taking it out on him now? Or maybe he'd been holding back before, worried that RJ would crumble like his father did if he placed too much pressure to perform on him?

RJ didn't know the answer, but he knew that he'd be passing the ball during the next half. They retook the field. Before RJ was even out on the field, the defense intercepted a Sunny Cal State pass and ran it back for a touchdown. It was suddenly 7-0. RJ knew that his own performance wouldn't be noticed as much now, since State was already winning. Someone else had broken the monotony of the game.

RJ stepped out onto the field. The ball snapped to him, and he looked for a player to hit. Kevin was running full-tilt down the field, which wasn't part of the play at all. He was supposed to run past the first-down line, then run right. Instead, he was running as fast as he could down the field.

RJ was able to calculate where Kevin would be, and fired the ball. The pass squarely hit Kevin, who seemed like he'd been expecting the ball the entire time, and it was only a few yards to a touchdown. The crowd went wild for the pass—cheering loudly and stomping on the stands. RJ walked off the field with two other players. When RJ saw Kevin on the bench, he walked over to him.

"What the hell was that?" RJ said without any compliments on the play.

"After the locker-room speech, I knew you'd be looking to hit a long pass. Why not pass it to me?"

"So you just ignored the play we agreed on?"

Kevin shrugged. "I know you. That talk of bowl games was going to make you do something big. So I just helped you out."

RJ rolled his eyes. Yes, he wanted to do something impressive for the fans and the reporters.

RJ didn't like that Kevin was anticipating what he wanted, rather than listening to what RJ told him to do. Kevin knew the darker side of RJ's ambition and fed on it, just as he had when he'd offered him drugs to show him that he could be an athlete and a good student.

"Next time, listen to what I say, not what you think I'm going to want. That's too dangerous."

Kevin saluted him and turned away to watch the game.

Toward the end of the fourth quarter, RJ was pulled from the game so that the backup quarterback could get some play time. RJ didn't mind too much, though he'd wished for more opportunities like the 50-yard pass. It felt good, even though Kevin went about it all wrong.

RJ left the locker room and headed back to the dining hall. No one from his family was at the game, and Mya was still working on a few projects for the end of the semester. RJ hadn't heard from his parents since he went home to talk to them last weekend. It was even more unusual that his grandfather hadn't called him yet. He wondered if his parents had told Grandpa about their conversation. It would explain the silence.

RJ noticed one of the agents, the one with the linebacker's build, standing outside the dining hall. Coach had been very explicit about staying away from agents and their offers. RJ was keeping the other conditions for his probation, so he planned on staying away from agents as well.

"RJ, how are you? I haven't talked to you lately. I just wanted to check in with you."

RJ nodded but didn't speak at first. He wanted to be clear about what he was going to say first. "I'm doing fine. Things have just been busy."

"I hear you. It's that time of year and all. Between finals and the bowl games, it's a hard time to be an athlete."

RJ remained silent. He wasn't sure what the purpose of this conversation was. He kept waiting for the other shoe to drop, but it remained on the agent's foot. They made small talk for a few minutes. Then the agent said, "So do you need any more papers to finish out the year?"

RJ looked at him. "That was you? You gave me that?"

The agent smiled. "No, but I heard rumors about it. You just confirmed those rumors. Thank you very much."

"Well, I didn't use it," RJ lied, sounding more like a child than an adult.

"I'm sure you didn't, because you're an upstanding young man." The agent's smile grew as he spoke. "Upstanding young men would never dream of doing such things, would they?"

RJ smiled back. "No, they wouldn't." His mind was racing. Did someone overhear him talking to Kevin about the paper? Had Kevin been talking about him behind his back? What exactly would happen if he got caught? He might fail the class and be expelled from school. He'd definitely lose his scholarship. RJ tried not to show his anxiety. The man was just chatting about his entire future, as if it were the weather.

"Then perhaps you'll tell me how upstanding this is?" The agent pulled out his phone and pressed a few buttons. He showed RJ the screen, which displayed a photograph of RJ from the night he passed out. It must have been taken a few minutes before he lost consciousness.

Another photo showed him throwing up, barely missing a pedestrian. In a second one, he was hanging onto a trash bin to keep from falling. In a third, he was falling to the ground.

The photos were graphic and required no explanation. Someone had taken photos of him during his weakest moments.

"Not too upstanding. More like falling down," the agent snickered. "I was just wondering what drugs were in your system that night? I bet the NCAA would like to know as well."

"It was alcohol. Just too much to drink."

"Uh-huh, you can tell them that." The man's eyes lost their twinkle. They were hard and cold now. RJ guessed that an agent had to be tough to fight for a client, but he never thought that an agent would fight against a potential one, too.

"I don't get this. What exactly do you want here? I'm just hearing a lot of speculation and rumors. I'm kind of in a hurry for dinner, if you don't mind."

"I'm just reminding you that a good agent will help you with PR issues. Keeping an athlete's reputation intact is a very vital part of my business. These pictures are minor, compared to what I deal with these days. But I'm here for you, RJ. You just need to sign with my agency, and I'll do the rest."

Now the other shoe had dropped. He'd been lured into a sense that he was in charge of his own future. However, that illusion was just as false as the one that he'd been in charge of his past. His grandfather had molded him in the past, and now this agent apparently wanted to mold him for the next decade.

RJ thought that he'd be his own person as an adult, but that didn't appear to be the case. He'd still be under the thumb of an agent, most likely this one. RJ wasn't sure of the purpose of blackmailing a player into signing with an agent. After he was pro, he'd have to talk to a lawyer to find out if those offenses would be punishable by the NCAA. He doubted it, but he could find out.

"So what's it going to be?" The agent put his phone back into his pocket, and pulled out some papers. "The university or my agency? If these photos go public, you might even get kicked out of the NCAA."

RJ knew that he had to stall, but he didn't know how to get out of this problem. "Can I at least talk this over with my girlfriend? I need to get her input before I make important decisions."

The agent nodded and laughed. "Sure, go ahead and do that now. Her opinion won't matter after you hit the big time, so you might as well pretend like you give a crap about it now."

"Hey, I don't appreciate talk like that. I love her."

"Sure you do. Just do what's best for everyone, and get drafted this season. I'll take my 25%, and we'll all be happy," the agent smirked.

"Wait, 25%? I thought it was 15."

"It's 25% for the agents who have some juicy information to tell the NCAA. Those are my terms. Learn to like them, or prepare to say goodbye to your scholarship and your football career."

The agent walked off, whistling a tune. RJ started walking toward the dining hall again, even though he had no appetite anymore.

Chapter 15

RJ CALLED MYA as soon as he got back to the dorm. "What am I going to do? How do I get out of this situation?"

Mya sighed. "I wish you'd come to me first, baby. It would never have gotten this bad if you had."

They discussed all of the options available to them. They boiled down to two possibilities.

The first was to accept the agent's proposition, and live with the threat of blackmail until he retired from the NFL. They had no doubt that these threats would continue until RJ was no longer a source of revenue.

The second option was to quit. RJ had objections to this plan:

He would lose his scholarship, so he'd either have to leave or pay his own tuition with no cash—if any school would keep him, since there was a strict honesty code at State. He could be expelled for using someone else's paper as his own.

He'd be out of football forever. He'd lose his chances to play, since no school would willingly take on a cheat and a drug abuser.

They debated back and forth, but neither plan made them feel good. RJ thought about what Mark said about following his happiness. Both of these plans made him miserable, and he didn't want to spend his life like this.

RJ and Mya agreed to talk again later in the week. In all the drama of decision-making, RJ barely registered that State would be playing in the Cotton Bowl in two weeks. Final exams flew by. With the help of a tutor, RJ did well on his tests, and got straight B's that semester. He was pleased with the results, even though he wanted to get an A in English—the class that his friend taught, and that his mother loved.

After school wound down, Coach put them on a constant regimen of practicing and running for the bowl game. He wanted to add another trophy to his impressive case of awards.

RJ felt bad for him. He knew that the agent was expecting a decision soon. If he chose to leave before the game, Coach might spend his last few years without another bowl win, especially if RJ's foibles came to light. Then they could be sanctioned, and ineligible for any bowl games.

On the Tuesday before the bowl game, RJ twisted his ankle again. He felt the pain shoot through his leg, and he immediately knew what he'd done. He didn't say anything to the team doctor or Coach about the situation. It was the end of practice, and he just wanted to go home and rest. He was in prime condition, except for the ankle, and he thought that rest would help it.

The next morning, the ankle wasn't much better. He could walk without a limp if he tried, but it didn't heal as fast as he thought it would.

An idea began to form in RJ's head. It wouldn't be an easy plan, but it was a third option that he and Mya hadn't discussed before. He called and talked to her about it. She wasn't in favor of it, but he knew that he could convince her. It would just take some time to make her see that it was a sacrifice they could all live with.

He called his grandfather as well. He hadn't talked to him for several weeks, but the old man was glad to hear from him. They talked for a while before RJ laid out what he wanted his grandfather to do. Surprisingly, the old man was agreeable as well. RJ felt good about his plan.

The team headed to Texas on Thursday. RJ still hadn't told anyone from State about his ankle. Coach didn't ask him about it in practice. RJ used a couple of the painkillers that the team doctor had supplied earlier. Since school was out, he had no worries about studying, and he could sleep 12 hours a day if he wanted to.

The first practice at Cowboys Stadium was insane. RJ was so excited about playing in an NFL stadium that he could barely remember his own name. It might be the closest he would ever get to the NFL now, but that was the consequence for what he'd done. He could live with it—if football wasn't taken away from him entirely.

The stadium was huge, exponentially larger than State's. (And even that stadium had intimidated him for weeks.) He gazed at the uppermost rows in the stadium, thinking that each of these rows would be filled with fans, along with the millions watching on television. The sheer size of it thrilled him. RJ wondered if he would ever be back here again.

He'd made up his mind about his plan. Mya still didn't like it, not one bit. But she agreed that it was better than some of the other options they'd discussed. This plan would give them the best of both worlds. He practiced with the team again that day, and iced his ankle that night.

The next day was a full day of practice on the field. RJ took in every minute of the experience, knowing that he wouldn't get many chances like this in his life. He wanted to savor every second, even the minutes when Coach had them running full-tilt in their uniforms. The Texas winter was chilly, but the uniforms made for a warm day. RJ could barely walk by the time he was finished for the day.

Coach stopped him on the way to the bus. "Are you okay? What's going on? I thought I saw you limping before. Is that ankle still giving you problems?"

RJ shook his head. "No, just tired from all the running. Do you have a remedy for that?"

Coach smiled. "More running. I could have you run back to the hotel if you keep up that mouth."

RJ chuckled. "No thanks. I'm good."

He went home that evening and iced his ankle again. Tomorrow was the big game, and RJ knew that a lot depended on what he did, and how he did it. He planned for as many possible scenarios as he could, but he knew from experience that football required you to think on your feet. It would be impossible to know all the things that could happen.

The game started in the afternoon, so people across the country could tune into the bowl game. RJ slept in, then got up in time for the morning practice. He was sharing a room with two other guys, but neither one of them was Kevin (which was a good thing). He'd have been tempted to share his plan with his roommate, but with these strangers, he was happy to just keep his mouth shut. They only said something to RJ when they wanted him to change the channel with the remote he was holding.

RJ heard the roar of the crowd as soon as he stepped on the field. It was overwhelming. He waved to the crowds, and smiled under his helmet at the number of people present. It was overwhelming. He still managed to enjoy it, hoping that he could recall every second of the game later in his life. His father had been to one bowl game, and now RJ could say the same.

The game started with the University of Cedar Rapids on offense. RJ was actually glad that he didn't have to play first. This time gave him a few minutes to acclimate himself to the stadium and the crowd. He recalled his first game at State, and how he wasn't able to hear his teammates during the huddle. He couldn't imagine what he would have done if his first game was of this magnitude. Maybe that was why the NFL wanted athletes to go through the college system before playing in the big time.

The time came for RJ to take the field. He was so revved up that he could barely feel the twinges in his ankle with every step. He was glad for the adrenaline: It helped him get past the nervousness and pain. Otherwise, his task would be so much harder.

The first down was simple: The ball snapped, and RJ passed it. Cedar Rapids was not prepared for a rapid offense, so RJ completed the second first down before they were ready. Their nerves were showing.

Two more first downs, and RJ threw for a touchdown. He walked back off the field, feeling good about himself. He'd scored in a bowl game, which was something he'd dreamed about doing since he was a child. The rush from accomplishing a childhood dream was overwhelming, and he grinned as he sat down on the bench.

But Cedar Rapids was determined, and they made it back to the 30-yard line.

RJ went back out on the field, but was shut down without making it to the first down this time. Apparently, Cedar Rapids was finding its feet. They weren't going to be a pushover in this game.

By the half, State still had the lead. The score was 14-6. Coach seemed pretty happy with the results so far. The locker-room speech was full of ire, but he didn't call anyone out. And he certainly didn't accuse RJ of not trying his best. For that, the quarterback was grateful.

The second half started with more of the same. Plenty of plays shut down, and lots of switching from offense to defense.

The start of the fourth quarter changed everything. With the third down, RJ saw his opportunity. The Cedar Rapids line had opened up about four feet, leaving RJ room to run the ball. This was his chance.

RJ tucked the ball under his arm and began to run. He had barely crossed the line of scrimmage when two of

Cedar Rapids players realized what happened. They spun, and started chasing RJ down the field. RJ put his all into it, feeling the pain in his ankle as he ran. A searing feeling began radiating up his leg. Each step became a jolt of agony. Yet he kept running.

At the seven-yard line, RJ felt the hand of a player on his jersey. On the two-yard line, he felt the brunt of an opponent hitting him hard. The other player struck as well. RJ pushed his body, stretching as far as he could. The pain in his leg became unbearable. Tears welled up in his eyes now. The pain had taken over his body.

RJ and the ball made it over the goal line. The crowd went wild, excitedly cheering for the touchdown, which all but cemented State's victory. The two players stood, but RJ was still lying on the ground. He couldn't stand anymore. He couldn't walk. He held the ball like a teddy bear, and just prayed for the pain to end.

The crowd went silent, as State's fans realized what the touchdown had cost them. Coach appeared above RJ, asking him what was wrong.

RJ croaked out, "It's my ankle. Something went wrong with my ankle. I can't use it at all." Kevin showed up, and offered him an arm to stand with. However, RJ knew that even with support, he'd never make it back to the bench.

The medics came out to the goal line. The game must have stopped for a moment. They looked at his leg and his foot. Nothing else seemed to be damaged. RJ could have told them that. The wave of pain crashed over him again, but it was worse this time.

The first medic administered a shot, which barely relieved the pain. RJ heard one of them say something about his Achilles tendon, which is what RJ had suspected from the moment he went down. The pain was too intense to be much else. Even a break would have been less painful.

They hoisted him onto the gurney, strapped him down, and carried him off the field. As he made his way to the locker room, the crowd gave him a standing ovation. The clapping sounded like thunder.

Before RJ passed out, he waved at the crowd, wishing them well.

Epilogue: Six Years Later

THE FOUR-YEAR-OLD GIRL grabbed a book and began to read it. She grabbed two more, and slid all three under her arm. She waited patiently while her parents were upstairs talking. She heard them laugh and say things that didn't make sense to her, but that was okay. Grownups did that. She opened the front door and went out to the front porch, where she sat down to read the first book. She wanted to savor them, so she read them slowly. Today would be a long day.

She'd nearly finished the first book when her parents arrived at the door. They were both dressed up, which is why they'd encouraged her to pick out a dress for the occasion. She wasn't sure what the big deal was. Daddy had a new job, but it was a lot like his old job. Why make a fuss?

RJ picked up his little girl and gave her a kiss. "How are you doing, Pumpkin? I love you."

She smiled at him. "I know."

"What are you reading?" he asked, putting her down. He knew better than to get between her and her books. Shrieking ensued. Alone, she was almost louder than a packed stadium.

She held up the book, which RJ knew for a fact that she'd read at least twenty times. She was like that. She didn't mind rereading a book. His mother claimed that she'd been the same way when she was a child.

Mya came out, looking incredible. She was wearing a formal dress, and RJ thought she looked like a movie star. She moved easily and gracefully—like she wore that attire every day. RJ gave her a kiss, and turned to move toward the car. His limp was more pronounced when he made a quick turn, but he'd grown used to it.

After the bowl game, RJ had learned that he'd snapped his Achilles tendon. The ankle movements had made the strain on it worse. And eventually, it had given way to the stress of a 50-yard run.

His original plan had just been to exacerbate his ankle injury to take a year or two off. He thought that would be enough time for the pressure to disappear. The agent would take it as a sign that he needed to leave him alone. RJ knew that such a move would have impacted his chances at a career in the NFL, but it seemed like the best option.

An injured player would be of little use to an agent, and RJ doubted that this agent would sabotage an injured player just because he could. If he did, his reputation would be at stake. The agent wouldn't have kicked RJ while he was already down. It would have been a bad break for RJ, but who would have thought that he'd done that, just to escape from an agent's clutches?

The tendon damage was unexpected, but it completed his plan in a firmer way. However, the chances of ever playing professional football disappeared that day. After his surgery and rehabilitation, RJ still had a limp that made running difficult for longer than a minute or so. He tried his best to fully recover, but it wasn't meant to be.

Of course, the end of his football career meant the end of his scholarships. Grandpa Robinson agreed to take some of the items he'd finagled from Edward Donley, and turn them into cash for RJ. The gifts and goods were enough to pay for most of RJ's tuition. And he found a part-time job that helped pay the bills.

RJ looked at his family. He could easily understand how his father decided that his wife and child were his priorities. After RJ's junior year, he and Mya decided to get married. She finished up her schooling a year early by taking extra classes and working weekends. When her friend Mike started an IT consulting business, she was the first person he hired. She was earning enough to support both of them.

As RJ's graduation approached, he struggled with what to do. Mya flew across the country on a regular basis, and offered to move them to a warmer climate, in the hopes that heat would help heal RJ's ankle. However, he didn't want to be that far from home. Even though most of his friends from State had graduated or moved on to other football teams, he still felt at home there.

So they got married at State. RJ actually asked Kevin to be his best man. Mya asked Mike to step up for her, and he agreed. Kevin's girlfriend caught the bouquet, and RJ spent the evening telling him all the things he had to look forward to. For once, he was the expert with women, and Kevin was the amateur.

This development didn't make RJ's decision about a career any easier. Even though he took a number of difficult classes, they didn't add up to a great career choice.

Mark was now working on his doctorate. So he talked to RJ about following a path that would make him happy. Mark suggested several books, implying that he already had an idea about what he thought he should do. But he didn't make outright suggestions. He wanted RJ to come to his own conclusions, based on his guidance.

However, Coach was much more straightforward. "Why don't you come on as an offense coach?" he asked one day while they were having lunch. RJ never told Coach about the paper or the agent. In the minds of everyone except Mya and his grandfather, RJ had accidentally suffered a career-ending injury at the bowl game. There was no reason to tell everyone else. RJ still worried that someone would find out and report it. But as time wore on, it became less and less likely that anyone would.

RJ was working part-time at the stadium, but at times, he felt more like a glorified water boy than a member of the coaching staff. However, he knew that the offensive coaches at State could use all the help they could get. With the proper preparation, the players could be so much more.

Mya and RJ discussed it at length. He still wanted to be involved with football in some way, and this opportunity would allow him to work in football as long as he wanted.

Mark agreed with RJ's decision to take the job, pointing out that all the books he'd recommended talked about seizing opportunities, "Too many people don't know a good thing, my friend. You have a great chance. Don't blow it."

RJ and Mya's little girl was born one year after they got married. They named her Linda after someone in Mya's family.

Mya was fine living near State. She was able to find an exceptional daycare for Linda when she was traveling.

RJ was actually relieved that Linda was a girl who wasn't interested in sports. It saved RJ the trouble of being a sports parent who worried about his child's performance every week. There would be no discussions about football, universities, and scholarships. Mya and RJ's mother frequently read to Linda, and between the two of them, she became a precocious reader.

Parenting became RJ, and he found himself feeling like a parent to each member of the offensive team at State. It was awkward at first, since some of them knew his reputation as a player. But after a few years, the new players only knew him by his reputation as a coach.

RJ was excited. He and Mya buckled Linda into her car seat and headed to the university for the ceremony. The details had all been ironed out weeks earlier, but the school wanted to have a PR moment. So RJ said he'd do it with Coach, who quickly agreed with a smile.

It was still early when they arrived, but some members of the press had already shown up for the ceremony. "What's all this about?" one of the reporters from ESPN shouted to RJ.

RJ just waved and helped Linda carry her books into the stadium. She'd been here plenty of times, enough to build up a routine. She picked out some books to bring, and RJ promised not to take up too much time. She was always very careful to ensure that he made this promise.

Coach was there, already at the podium. RJ looked around. He was shocked to see his parents in attendance. That was the last thing he'd expected, but there they were in the third row—waiting for the news to go public.

RJ spied his grandfather, who sat in another row by himself. The aftermath of the injury led to some harsh words between his father and grandfather. Things hadn't completely resolved, but RJ saw signs of them working things out.

Kevin was also in attendance. He laughed and clapped RJ on the back. "Never thought I'd see you like this. How does it feel to be on the other side? Are you going to tell them to do what you say, and not what you do?"

"I could ask the same of you," RJ said. "Your wedding is coming up in a few weeks. I'll have to bite my tongue, so I won't snicker during the vows."

"Go ahead and laugh, buddy. But I'm a one-woman man now."

RJ smiled and headed back up to the podium with Coach. Kevin took a seat next to a pretty reporter, who got a quote from him for her story. He played for the Vikings, but he wasn't on the field much. In fact, he barely hung on from season to season, so he needed all the PR he could get.

Several more reporters came into the room. RJ looked to Coach, who nodded. He tapped on the mic and started speaking, "I'd like to present the man who's been State's head coach for the past 32 years. He's a legend at this school and in the conference: Coach Mosby."

A few hands flew up from the reporters, but Coach chose to ignore them. "Thank you. A few months ago, I decided that my time here was done. I've worked here for 40 years. It's time to pass the torch, and let a younger man bring new, fresh ideas to the team. I've had the pleasure of knowing this young man for several years, and I knew his family before he was born. I've watched this man grow and mature, and I want to let him do the same for young men as they enter State—for an education, and for football. His family is good people. Ladies and gentlemen, beginning with next year's season, State's new head football coach will be RJ Robinson."

THE END

Acknowledgments

FIRST AND FOREMOST, I'd like to thank my mother. Throughout years of battling her own health issues, she always found a way to support me. Her unfaltering love, encouragement, and investment in my dreams created the foundation for the person that I am today.

And to my father: You've proven that people should follow their dreams, no matter what, and that it's never too late to step up to the plate. You were there when I needed you most, and you inspire me to be the best man that I can possibly be.

Grandparents, I'm not sure if you'll ever know the influence you've had on me over the years. You were always there for me, investing whatever you possibly could to help make my goals achievable.

And, of course, my wonderful siblings. You are the best bunch of sisters a guy could ever hope for, and I want to thank you for simply being you. Never change. But I'd like to acknowledge one sister in particular; you know who you are. Together, we've proven that persistence and dedication always prevail, so we should never give up. I love you.

Lastly, I'd really like to thank all of those people who normally get overlooked on this page. This book is about people investing in others, so I'd like to honor that.

Thank you to my stepmother, aunts, uncles, coaches, friends, and other family... Sometimes, even just a simple, kind gesture can make a difference and give someone the push they need to keep going in the right direction.

Made in the USA
Columbia, SC
10 July 2018